A Botin ...

Originally from London, Surrey-based author, Jacquelynn Luben has published two successful non-fiction books and many articles, but is equally at home with fiction, having written numerous short stories. Coming late into further education, she gained a degree from Surrey University in 2002, with a dissertation on the Harry Potter series.

To Irene,

My fellow writer,
with best wishes

Jackie

1st Oct 05

Also by Jacquelynn Luben

The Fruit of the Tree
Published by Nelson Houtman

Other books by Goldenford Publishers

On the Edge   Esmé Ashford
The Moon's Complexion   Irene Black

A Bottle of Plonk

Jacquelynn Luben

Goldenford Publishers Ltd
Guildford

First published in Great Britain in 2005 by

Goldenford Publishers Limited

The Old Post Office

130 Epsom Road Guildford

Surrey GU1 2PX

Tel: 01483 563307

Fax: 01483 829074

www.goldenford.co.uk

Printed and bound by Antony Rowe Ltd, Eastbourne

ISBN 0-9531613-3-1

Acknowledgements

I should like to thank the members of Guildford Writers' Circle, who read this story and whose comments enabled me to produce a much improved book, and all at Goldenford Publishers for their efforts in getting A Bottle of Plonk into shape.

Contents

Chapter 1: Sons & Lovers

(Sunday night, Spring Bank Holiday)

The remains of the dinner littered the table, together with two bottles of wine, one empty, one unopened. The dimmed lights in the living room softened the uncluttered lines of the small flat. Two candles cast shadows transforming the faces of the couple as they held hands across the table.

Julie Stanton, with her slanted green eyes, looked almost Oriental in a tangerine coloured caftan. The effect was enhanced by the spiky black hair framing her face. Her expression was transparent, and the glow not just from the wine.

'This is such a special day, Richard. I think we ought to commemorate it.'

She withdrew her hand from Richard's and, with a pen left on the table, she carefully executed a heart and arrow on the label of the unopened wine.

'Very artistic,' Richard commented. 'No wonder you were the star of our art class. Shall we open it now?'

Julie didn't answer. She was concentrating on adding the date to the label, 28th May 1989.

1

'If you're going to put it in the wine cellar and open it in twenty years' time, you should have chosen something better than this supermarket plonk,' Richard commented.

'You don't understand. Tomorrow, I'm going to paint the bottle. I'm going to stand it in the centre of the table on a silver tray, and when we look at the painting in twenty years time, we'll remember what an important date it was.'

Richard laughed softly. 'Well in that case, let's round off the evening...' He reached for the corkscrew.

Julie smiled at him. She was satiated by the meal, and foolishly happy at being with the man she loved. She embellished the heart with 'J loves R' in minuscule letters and put her hand on his.

'We'll have it after...' she said, the rest of her words lost, as she leant across the table to kiss him.

'Shameless hussy,' Richard said, pulling her closer. 'You've been listening to those delinquents you teach.'

Julie laughed. She thought it was odd that sitting here with the man she adored, she was one person - a young woman, vulnerable at times - while to her class of seven year olds, she was 'Miss', very confident and at twenty-five, very old.

'My mother always told me not to get involved with school teachers. Mind you that was when I was nine.'

Julie frowned a little, and dropped her arms to her side.

'Your mother's not going to like me, Richard.'

'What are you talking about?'

'Must we go to Exeter this week? I'm worried about meeting her.'

'There's no need to be. You can control a horde of felons. My mother should be a piece of cake.'

'It's not as if we're engaged. Why do we have to be so formal?'

Richard sighed. 'You know I go down there every month. I don't want to keep leaving you behind.'

'She wouldn't listen when you phoned and told her I was moving in here. And she didn't reply when you wrote and told her about me.'

'There wasn't anything to say. I just told her I'd be bringing you down at the end of the week. She'll be fine when we get there.'

'She's going to think I'm not good enough for you.'

'You're being ridiculous. Why are you making a drama out of this?'

'Because you've been to a posh public school and university and all that, and I went to the local comprehensive and teachers' training college.'

'You know none of that matters to me. I love you as you are.'

'But your mother won't.'

Richard took her hand again and squeezed it. 'Look. Let me tell you something about my mother. She jumps to conclusions very quickly but, after a little while, she settles down. She's also a bit protective of her children.'

'In what way, protective?'

'She was married rather a long time before Liz and I showed up. She was forty when I was born and Liz came along a year later. Obviously, she thought she wasn't going to have any kids. Then my father died suddenly. That made us more special, I suppose.' He cleared his throat. 'In fact, she hasn't really taken to any of my girl-friends. '

'And what about your sister? Liz?'

'Liz had the same sort of problems, when she brought her boy-friends home. Particularly Gary. Which is rather a shame, because he's the one that Liz ended up marrying. Mother created quite a fuss about that. She does get at poor old Gary quite a lot. But mostly he seems to be able to deal with it.'

Julie was far from reassured. 'But will I be able to?'

'Of course you will. Now I don't want you to worry about it. Let's enjoy the next few days.'

Julie relaxed at the thought of the half-term holiday ahead. There would be plenty to do in the little flat, squeezing in her possessions. She would collect the rest of her things from her bed-sit during the week.

'Did you see what I brought with me?' she said. 'Your painting.'

'Oh, that. Why didn't you leave it in the flat with Sue and Sally?'

'Because it's our only shared possession. Perhaps we could hang it now? It'll be symbolic.'

Richard's expression changed.

'You must be mad, Julie. I'm not going to do that tonight. It'll take me ages.'

His lack of enthusiasm spurred her on.

'Don't be silly. Why, my brothers could put something like that up in five minutes.' The dig was to punish him for his mother's misdemeanours.

His blue eyes flashed. He got up and found some tools. She was aware that he was ill at ease and clumsy with a hammer in his hand.

'Gently, Richard.'

He glared at her. 'Do you want to take over?'

We're going to row over nothing, Julie thought. This shouldn't have happened on our first night together.

She mollified him, 'No of course not. Just be careful.'

Steadying the nail with his fingers, he aimed a blow at the wall. The lights flickered and went out.

'What have you done now?'

'Goodness knows.' replied Richard. 'I must have hit a wire in the wall.'

'Pull the nail out, then.' It occurred to her that he might not know how. 'Pull it out with the claw on the back of the hammer.'

There was enough light in the room for that at least, but after this effort, Richard, it seemed, had had enough. 'Well that's it. Let's go to bed and worry about it tomorrow?'

'Don't tease.'

His voice became tender.

'In bed with you, I shall have everything I need.' Then he added, 'And there'll be less likelihood of us tripping over something and killing ourselves.'

Julie laughed, 'Stop joking and deal with it.'

'This is no joke. Put me in an office with the FT, and I'll make an illuminating comment. But when it comes to how things work, I haven't the foggiest. My plugs try to electrocute me; taps I've just washered leak all over me.'

Well, this was quite a revelation, thought Julie. You imagined you knew someone well enough to move in with them, and then they surprised you. Well, disappointed you, to be precise. Everyone in Julie's family could get themselves out of trouble. They were practical people, the Stantons. Richard was quite unlike them. Was it going to work?

Richard was continuing, 'If you want to play DIY games, go to B&Q on a Sunday. You'll find plenty of playmates.'

He was getting tense, she could tell. What did his impracticality matter? She'd always known he was a bit of a dreamer. She loved his sense of humour, his looks, his sex appeal, and his occasional romantic gestures.

She kissed his ear.

'I'd rather stick with you, my love. But we can't leave this. Let me try to fix it. I've learned a lot from Frank and Barry.'

'The more I hear of your accomplished brothers, the more I dread meeting them,' interrupted Richard.

'In that case, you ought to understand how I feel about your mother,' Julie said. Then relenting a little, she added, 'But you've no need to worry.' She placed a hand on his arm and tried to get her bearings in the semi-darkness. 'Frank is an absolute sweetie. You'll get on fine with him.' She squeezed his hand. 'And as for Barry, he's the original MCP and I avoid him like the plague. Anyway, this isn't the time to discuss it. Let me demonstrate my talents.'

'A great idea!' said Richard, still holding on to the hand, and succeeding in grabbing the rest of her. 'Why don't you?'

The light scent of his after-shave was clean and refreshing. The touch of his hand affected her like no one else's.

She hesitated, but resisted the temptation.

'You see, with the nail out, I may only need to reset the fuse,' she explained. But she knew it was more complex than that. She was being bloody-minded, all because she felt threatened by a woman she had never met. A woman who, in her mind, had taken on all the attributes of Maggie Thatcher.

She climbed the pair of rickety steps in the electrical cupboard, torch in hand, with her mind on what should have been the romantic end to the evening, which had now been delayed by her actions.

'How's it going?'

'The fuse box is a bit high up. What a pain it is to be vertically challenged. Ouch, I think I've caught my caftan on a nail. It'll never be the same again.'

'You poor thing. I'll buy you a new caftan. But don't injure yourself. I can't get another you.'

'I'll be careful,' said Julie, smiling in the darkness at his words. She'd sort this out and everything would be fine.

A hollow banging sound penetrated the dark cupboard. 'What was that noise? Is there someone at the door?'

'Not sure,' replied Richard, feeling his way along the hall. 'We're not expecting anyone.'

He opened the door.

The street lights illuminated the face of a small woman in the entrance. Violet Webb stood before him, erect and dignified, looking taller than her five feet.

'Mother!' he said shocked. 'What are you doing here?'

'Why are you in darkness?'

'We were trying to hang this picture. I must have grazed a wire. Julie's doing a repair job.'

'Julie?'

He took her arm and escorted her through the dark hall.

'I think I've found the fuse!' came Julie's voice from the electrical cupboard. 'Can you help me?'

'Just a second,' Richard called. 'That's Julie,' he told his mother. 'Remember I told you she was moving in.'

Lights suddenly flashed on, but Julie's success was followed by a crash and a scream, and she descended from the electrical cupboard, pulling the steps down with her as she fell, landing directly in front of Richard and his mother. Her caftan was ripped down one side revealing a white flash of underwear and a great deal of leg.

The older woman looked down at her, and the blue eyes might have been carved from marble.

'I think your friend needs some help, Richard.'

Julie struggled to reinstate her clothing. 'I'm all right,' she said, feeling a bruise forming at the side of her face. Her eyes were smarting, partly from pain and partly from humiliation at being stared at by that ice-blue gaze.

Her immediate impression was that Mrs Webb was the archetypal English lady, with silver hair, and a youthful pink and white complexion, more like Barbara Cartland than Thatcher. But those wide eyes undoubtedly hid a steely character. Only the hands, gnarled and distorted by arthritis, and the stick that supported the frail legs, gave a clue to her advancing years.

Richard relinquished his mother, disentangled Julie from the steps and helped her to her feet.

'Oh Richard. I've left a bag with one or two things at your front door,' Mrs Webb interposed. 'Go and get it for me, would you?' She limped towards the living room, where the offending painting sat on the floor beneath its proposed position.

'Go on. I'm all right,' said Julie. She freed herself, followed the other woman into the living room, and she too sat herself down to recover. The painting, conspicuous in the small room, drew their attention. Violet turned to look at Julie, their eyes met and then Violet's returned to the picture.

Violet Webb didn't say a word, as she viewed the subject's legs, so recently observed in the flesh, the round pink curves topped by Julie's face, the lithe young body decorated with flowers and chiffon scarves, but otherwise, very little else.

Then she looked carefully at Julie again. 'Are you sure that's suitable for the living room?' she asked, and from the way she said it, Julie felt as if she had been portrayed on a giant size page three in one of the popular tabloids. She marvelled at the fact that in a single sentence Mrs Webb had managed to encapsulate her disdain for the painting, her antipathy for her son's relationship with its model, and her total dislike of Julie herself.

Nevertheless, Julie protested, 'Richard is really talented - he ought to be painting for a living instead of carrying out boring audits.'

'Your faith is touching, my dear,' said Violet. 'But money is a great motivator. You must surely have been in that situation yourself, when you modelled for Richard's art class.'

'I didn't model for the class,' Julie replied, startled. 'This was between me and Richard. But in any case, I really don't feel there should be any stigma attached to that. Someone has to model, otherwise ordinary people simply miss out on the opportunity to paint from life.'

'How very avant garde of you, my dear. I must say at my age, one longs for the days when a little was left unrevealed.'

'Really mother,' Richard intervened, having returned for the tail end of the conversation, with a large hold-all. 'If everyone was so narrow-minded, we would have missed out on goodness knows how many paintings and sculptures.'

'Please don't start an argument, Richard. You know I can't stand it. Elizabeth is just the same. Losing her temper at any little thing. I can't put up with that. That's why I've had to leave Exeter. I'll be staying here for a while.'

'It's impossible for you to stay here,' said Richard, horrified. 'Let me book a hotel room for you.'

'That's very kind of you, dear. But with my angina, I'm very reluctant to be abandoned with strangers. And since you seem to have worked out some way of accommodating er Judy,...'

Julie felt her temper rising, as Richard said, his face reddening, 'Julie! That's hardly the same, mother.'

'Oh really, dear. Why is that?'

'Well Julie and I are going...'

'.. are living together,' said Julie, seeing that Richard was going to spend all day thinking up delicate ways of phrasing their relationship.

'Yes, of course. I do admire your directness. You young people are so sensible and pragmatic nowadays. One hardly ever hears those old fashioned expressions like "living in sin",' Violet Webb murmured.

Not receiving any response, she added, 'One took it all so seriously in my day. So much better now, not to enter into any permanent commitments and to be able to end relationships, when they've served their purpose.'

Her eyes rested on Julie for a second or so too long, and Julie, astute enough to recognise all those little glances and pointed comments, aimed like tiny poison darts, got out of the firing range.

'I'll make some coffee,' she said.

'What a helpful girl,' said Violet, her voice just that little louder, now that it had to reach into the kitchen. 'And what a lovely figure she has - I can see why you find her attractive.'

Julie returned with coffee, placing the cup on a small table at Violet's side. The older woman took one or two sips.

'Is it decaffeinated, my dear? I'm afraid that ordinary coffee makes my heart race.'

Julie put her hand to her mouth. 'Oh, I'm sorry, I didn't think.'

'Well never mind, you weren't to know. I won't finish it, if you don't mind. Richard, I'm exhausted. The train journey has quite sapped my energy. If it's inconvenient, I'll gladly borrow your studio couch tonight, and until I get myself organised. I'm sure it will only be for a week or two.'

The little serene smile remained; the innocent eyes did not change expression, despite the perceptible stiffening of both the other occupants of the room.

'You can't possibly sleep on the couch, mother. You'll obviously have to sleep in my room,' said Richard, dutifully, his brow furrowed. Julie waited for him to include her in the arrangements, but he said nothing more, obviously daunted by his mother's presence, and finally, Julie got up, fighting back tears.

'There's really only one solution, Richard. I'll go back to Sally and Sue and stay there. You can give me a ring when you've got it sorted.'

Richard, looking impotent, could suggest no way to avert what Julie suggested.

'But what if no-one's up? I'll come with you and make sure you get in. Or perhaps it would be better if I slept on the floor here and you slept on the couch,' he floundered.

'I won't be locked out. They're having a party. You know they always have people over at the weekend. In fact, it'll probably be fun. I'll take them that bottle of wine as a peace offering.'

She saw the hurt expression on Richard's face as she mentioned the wine that was part of their special celebration. She had meant to wound him and she had succeeded.

'Anyway, you couldn't possibly come with me.' she continued, formally polite, as if she were addressing a stranger. 'You must sort out clean sheets and things for your mother! I'll give you a ring in a few days and see what you've arranged.'

She had not even unpacked her small suitcase, and she picked it up now, collected the wine and headed for the front door, forcing her lips into a twisted smile. He followed her out.

'I'm going to get really drunk now,' she said, kissing him lightly on the lips. The brief kiss, which threatened to last longer than either intended was arrested suddenly by a crash and a feeble shriek from Violet Webb.

'Oh dear, I've knocked the coffee over. Don't worry, I'll be all right.'

Richard turned his head abruptly and released his hold on Julie, 'Have you scalded yourself, mother?'

Julie's mouth tightened into a hard line of resignation.

'Go and make sure she's all right. I'll see you soon. Love you.' But the last whispered comment wasn't heard by Richard as he ran to assist his mother, who had knocked coffee over her dress and the floor - perhaps in an effort to get up - or perhaps not. The coffee was barely warm now and Violet was certainly not scalded. But even as Richard noticed that, he heard the front door slam.

Julie drove the little Fiat confidently through the London streets. She passed by Sally and Sue's flat and saw the brightly lit rooms, but despite what she had said, she was in no state for a party. She could have climbed the stairs straight to her room and ignored everyone, for she still had a key. But she drove on past the flat, out of central London. Perhaps a little bit of family atmosphere was what she needed.

The sign said three miles to Wimbledon and she continued along, not really needing to think about the journey. She had been looking forward to the week ahead - possibly the life ahead, shared with Richard. But perhaps she didn't really know him after all. Perhaps he wasn't the man for her. It was better to find out now. Tears were pricking at her eyelids and she was glad she was going to be amongst people who would make a fuss of her. Her own parents were too far away, but her brother, Frank, and his wife Janet would look after her.

She drew up outside a large comfortable looking house and peered at her watch. It was just before midnight, but the hall light was on. She went up to the front door and rang the bell.

Chapter 2: The Generation Game

(Sunday night and Bank Holiday Monday)

Frank Stanton came to the door in his dressing gown. Julie was used to his normal expression of tired resignation coupled with good humour, as he dealt with a range of family problems. Tonight though, he appeared unusually worried, and it seemed to Julie, as she stood in the shadowy doorway, clutching her bottle of wine in one hand and her suitcase in the other, that it was unconnected to her late appearance on the scene.

'Julie!' he exclaimed, and a smile lit up his face, taking away the middle-aged look that had developed.

Julie was suddenly very glad to see him. She enveloped him in a big hug, dropping her small suitcase, but retaining the wine.

Looking a little overwhelmed by her exuberance, Frank eventually disentangled himself and took her case from the floor.

'I've come to be a nuisance,' she said, her voice taking on little sister mode.

'So you're here to stay, are you?' he said. 'Claridges not good enough for you?' He sounded unsurprised, but resigned, Julie thought, but she knew with Frank she could get away with anything. 'And this bottle of wine's your peace offering, I assume? Thanks a lot, love, but next time, give us a half hour's warning.' He rested the bottle of wine on the hall table, next to the telephone. 'Actually, Janet and I were just having some cocoa. Let's get inside - you must be freezing in that - er - outfit.'

Julie walked past her reflection in the oval mirror and the light in the hallway showed up the bruised cheek and the rip in the caftan for the first time.

'Whatever's happened to you, Julie?' Frank exclaimed. 'Has someone attacked you?'

'I fell off a ladder, doing some DIY,' Julie replied, following him into the large kitchen. Janet was sitting at the kitchen table in a faded blue dressing gown, obviously concerned as to the identity of the midnight caller. Julie delivered more kisses and greetings. Janet's face, having registered relief at the familiar face, now gasped at Julie's unkempt appearance.

'What have you done to yourself, Julie? You look as if you've been in a battle. And it's so late.'

'It's not that boyfriend, is it?' growled Frank. 'I didn't think he was an aggressive character.'

'You needn't worry. That's not one of Richard's faults,' Julie said with a watery smile, sitting herself down at the kitchen table. She looked from one to the other. 'But I have got a problem, and I'd really appreciate it if I could stay for a couple of days, if you don't mind.'

'I'll make you some cocoa,' Janet said.

She took a mug from the Welsh dresser and, as if on auto-pilot, prepared the drink for Julie. Julie always thought that, with her curly brown hair, Janet looked young to have a daughter of eighteen, but she noticed now that fine lines were showing at the sides of Janet's eyes, and there was a weariness about her posture. It was obvious that something was on her mind.

Julie tried to lighten the atmosphere.

'Look, I'm sorry about this, but Richard's been invaded by his old bat of a mother. So I'm homeless and in need of some TLC.'

'I'm not sure I'm much use at that,' Janet said through tight lips.

Julie's smile faded. It was not the sort of response she would have expected from Janet.

'I don't want you to go to any trouble. The settee will do - or the floor.'

'Don't be silly,' Janet said stirring the cocoa and passing it to Julie. Her lips trembled slightly. 'I'm just not sure I'm a marvellous mother.'

She sat down, covering her face with her hands and started to weep silently.

'Oh Janet. What's happened?' Julie said startled. 'You're a wonderful person - and a wonderful mother. What's happened to upset you?'

'It's Caroline,' Frank said. His face, which was already showing dark stubble, distorted into a grimace, as he spoke of his daughter.

'Why don't you sit down Julie, and we'll tell you. We've been talking it through tonight - that's why we're still up. She rang last weekend and told us she was pregnant. Some chap she met at work. But the relationship's broken up - she's talking about an abortion. You can imagine how we feel.'

'It's like a nightmare, Julie,' sobbed Janet. 'I wake up each morning and hope for a minute that I've dreamed it. Why didn't she take precautions? I know things have changed over the years. But she's so young. I don't know which is worse - the idea of her ruining her life, saddling herself with a child at her age - or the thought of the abortion - my first grandchild.'

Julie started to speak, but Frank shook his head. He put his arm round his wife and led her up the stairs. Then he returned a few minutes later.

'Julie. No more tonight. Janet's had enough. She says the spare room bed's made up, and would you mind looking after yourself, just for now.'

Julie nodded. She didn't know what to say. All the well-aired comments about a woman's right to choose seemed inappropriate in this situation. So she said nothing - just hugged her brother with all the affection she felt for him. Then she finished her drink on her own, and went to bed.

* * *

When Julie came down in the morning, Janet was dressed. She was wearing a navy blue T-shirt and check trousers, and she looked cool and composed. When the two younger children had disappeared outside, Julie felt able to resume the conversation of the previous night, and the two women sat with their coffee at the stripped pine kitchen table.

'I'm really sorry about everything, Janet,' Julie said. 'Here's me - getting upset about my trivial little problem and you've got a real tragedy on your hands. I know how dreadful you must feel.'

'You *don't* know,' Janet said quietly. 'I've had no career - not like you. I've put the family before everything - and I'd do it all again if I could. The family's been my career. But now it seems I've failed at the only thing I've ever done.'

She ignored Julie's attempt to interrupt. 'The children are getting older; soon they won't need me, and I don't know what I'm supposed to do with my life. Frank says that it's time I had my own interests. A few weeks ago, I went along to an agency for some work - before all this happened - and I was scared, really scared.' She twisted her wedding ring on her finger.

'What happened?'

'It was just office work. They said they'd let me know. But they were so young. I felt completely out of touch - like an invader from Mars. I hoped desperately they'd say they didn't want me. To think that she can even contemplate an abortion. There are so many women longing for children... How did things go so wrong?'

Julie got up and poured herself some more coffee.

'What if she kept the baby?' she asked.

'I'd be very relieved. But it wouldn't be easy. She lives in a flat with two other girls. She works a twelve hour day. How could she possibly manage? A child minder, I expect.' Her face expressed her distaste. 'I hate the thought of a child being passed around like a parcel.'

'Do you think she'd come back home?' Julie asked, knowing the answer already. Caroline was rather like her in personality.

'She won't give up her career for anything. Or her independence. She's all self, that girl. And it's my fault.'

Julie stood up and put an arm round her sister-in-law. 'People aren't putty. I see it with the kids at school. Even in families, they turn out differently. Look at Frank and Barry - they're like chalk and cheese.'

'Oh, goodness. Barry and Linda. I'd quite forgotten. We're supposed to be going for a snack with them this evening. I haven't organised a baby-sitter or anything. Not that the kids really need one. But this business with Caroline has put everything else out of my mind.'

'I'll stay with the kids,' offered Julie. 'As long as I'm here, I might as well be useful.'

'Actually, Julie,' said Janet with a trace of her normal good humour. 'You know you're always welcome. But just how long are you staying?'

'If I could just crash down here for a few days - that would be wonderful. I've got a week's holiday. That's why I was moving in with Richard this weekend - until it all went pearshaped.'

Janet took a handkerchief from her pocket, and blew her nose hard. 'We'll make a nice lunch. Cheer us all up. You can give me a hand and you can tell me all about this silly squabble between you and Richard.'

Here in her own element, Janet was confident and efficient. She talked and worked at the same time. Together the sisters-in-law tidied the beds, peeled vegetables, prepared a roast and dessert, with Julie acting very much as a subordinate.

Julie watched Janet as she took a tray of drinks outside, where Frank was washing the car, and the younger children, Katie and James, were roller-skating. It seemed an idyllic picture of family life. Julie had a mental picture of Richard in a similar domestic scene. She suddenly wanted very much to hear his voice. She called out of the window that she was going to use the phone.

'Richard is out,' came Violet Webb's disembodied voice, entirely devoid of regret, 'Can I give him a message?'

Julie reeled off her telephone number and stressed that she was not after all staying with her ex-flatmates. But she could almost imagine Mrs Webb reducing her telephone number to confetti. She could hardly hide her disappointment at not being able to speak to Richard.

'No luck?' queried Janet, returning to the kitchen.

'No, it was the Wicked Witch of the West. I bet she doesn't give him the number.'

As if in response, the telephone rang.

'Perhaps that's him,' said Janet, 'You go and answer it.'

Julie felt that little flutter of nervous apprehension which incorporated hope, delight and fear in equal parts, as she skipped to the phone, but once again a female voice sounded at the other end.

'Auntie Julie, how are you?'

'Great, Caroline! Cut the "Auntie" for heaven's sake. How are *you*?'

She saw Janet's face change, her lips tense, as she heard her daughter's name.

At the other end of the phone, Caroline replied, 'I'm OK. I've had a bit of a problem. But I'm getting it sorted out. Can I speak to Mum please?'

Sorted out, thought Julie. What did that mean? An abortion? She handed the phone to Janet, and went outside to Frank, waiting until Janet joined them.

'She's coming home, Frank,' Janet said, turning to her husband. 'She'll be here this afternoon. She wants you to pick her up off the four thirty train.'

Frank put down his cloth, and placed his hands on Janet's shoulders. 'Don't say anything to the kids. You said they were going out this afternoon, anyway.'

'I hate keeping secrets from them.'

'Time enough to tell them when a decision's been made,' Frank said, his voice grim. 'And if there's no baby, perhaps not even then.'

After the ordeal of a lunch, during which Frank, Janet and Julie vied with each other in their efforts to be cheerful, Frank transported Katie and James to their friends, and later, he left once again to collect Caroline.

Janet and Julie waited, on tenterhooks, looking out of the sitting room window.

'Shall I disappear?' Julie asked, as Frank's car turned into the drive.

'No, please stay. She gets on so well with you.'

Frank was garaging the car as Caroline walked in. She looked young and vulnerable, in a baggy sweater and jeans, long, straight flaxen hair framing her small face. Close to tears, she hugged both her mother and Julie wordlessly. Nevertheless, her mouth looked set in a determined way and, when her father came in, she started talking straight away.

'I've just come to tell you. I've made my decision. I'm not going to have my life mucked up by having a baby. I've decided to have an abortion.'

Janet turned away and closed her eyes in pain.

'You'd better sit down and we'll talk about this,' Frank said, pacing backwards and forwards. 'You haven't told us anything about the man involved. Isn't he prepared to help you?'

'It was just a one night stand. I didn't see him again. He was working in the Futures market.'

'Fine future he's given you,' muttered Janet.

'And how about afterwards?' Frank said. 'It'll be too late to change your mind then.'

'Look, this is the hardest decision I've ever made,' Caroline said, her voice suddenly solemn.

'I already feel pregnant.' She got up again and turned to her mother. 'I just can't face the thought of being like you.'

'What do you mean?' Janet gasped.

'Trapped here, fulfilling your martyrdom,' Caroline snapped.

'I've never given that impression,' retorted Janet angrily. 'I've always been very happy at home.'

'Well, maybe you have, but I can tell you it's never appealed to me for one second. Suburbia. Baking cakes. Hoovering. I couldn't get away fast enough.'

'Well, it's a pity you didn't think of all that when you got yourself pregnant. If you wanted a career - and I've never criticised you for that - why were you so careless?'

'You didn't say what it was really like.'

'I've always tried to prepare you.'

'Of course. The perfect mother. You gave me lectures. You told me about sex as if it was some sacrifice you had to make in order to have babies.' Janet flushed and looked down at her feet. 'You didn't tell me it was fun,' Caroline went on. 'I didn't go out looking for sex. I didn't go prepared. I just went for a meal with a nice guy. I enjoyed talking to him and he was good looking. We had wine and I wanted to stay in his company. When we went back to his flat, I thought I could handle it. I didn't know I'd be overwhelmed. You never told me what it was like.'

'Some things are difficult to talk about to your children,' said Janet, twisting the frill of a cushion nervously around her fingers.

'Well, you should have tried harder,' said Caroline. 'Don't you think so, Julie?'

Julie hesitated. She was fond of them both. In her own view, she was the last person to make judgements, yet here they both were waiting for her words as if for the wisdom of Solomon.

'I think you're talking a lot of nonsense, Caroline. You're an eighteen year old adult. You've chosen to leave home and take on a responsible job. You've made a mistake and now you're running back to Mummy so she can be the scapegoat. You learn from your friends, Caroline. That's the way it is and that's the way it's always been. I can't remember my mum giving me a lecture on the joys of sex.'

Frank gave a bitter laugh at this particular image.

Julie carried on, surer now of her ground. Being a modern woman was one thing. Passing the buck was another.

'As you said, you thought you could handle the situation and you couldn't. It happens. You were just unlucky that you got pregnant. The question is not who's to blame, but how you are going to deal with it.'

She paused, feeling satisfaction at seeing some relief on Janet's face.

'I've told you what I'm going to do,' Caroline replied, her expression that of a sulky five-year-old.

'Caroline, what is it that worries you most - having it or looking after it?' Janet asked slowly.

'I told you, I don't want to hurt it. I just don't want to look after it,' replied Caroline, her lips trembling.

'Why don't you have it adopted or fostered?' asked Julie.

'Mum wouldn't let me, would you?' replied Caroline and indeed her mother was shaking her head, saying, 'No, no.'

Then Janet added, surprisingly calmly, 'Of course, the answer's staring us in the face.'

'Is it?'

'It's sticking out a mile. I'll look after the baby. You know I'm good with children. I was saying to you this morning, Julie, I'd do it all over again, wasn't I?'

'Yes, you were,' said Julie, slowly digesting this. 'But...'

'Well, there you are then. I'll be the childminder.'

'Now hold on,' Frank started, but Caroline did not let him finish.

'How could I live with that? You'd always be pushing it down my throat. Doing your martyr bit. Like you've done all my life.'

'You've got your mother all wrong,' said Julie angrily.

'Yes, you're right, Julie. Of course, I should have realised. It's a damned easy way to get another lovely baby, isn't it, without all the nasty messy palaver beforehand.'

Frank, whose face was showing increasing anger at the female exchanges, now rounded on his daughter, gripping her shoulders hard. 'Caroline, I won't have you speaking to your mother like that.'

For a moment it looked as if he was going to shake her. Then he put his hands back down to his sides and with controlled fury, he continued. 'You're talking to your mother as if she's the one who's in trouble. If you can't treat her civilly, then get out now!'

Caroline's face flamed at this unusually angry reaction from her father.

'All right. I'll go,' she said, her voice shaking.

Janet jumped up and put a protective arm round her. 'Don't be ridiculous, Frank. She always does hit out when she's upset. You don't think I'm going to take any notice of all that nonsense.' Turning to Caroline, her voice softened, 'We only want what's best, love. Best for you and the baby. It's not selfishness, I promise you. Don't take a step you'll regret all your life.'

Caroline's lips trembled and tears started running down her cheeks. 'I'm sorry, Mum. I shouldn't have said those things.'

Janet, her face wet with tears in a mirror image of her daughter's, put both arms round her and hugged her.

'So that's decided then.'

'If you really think it would work out, I don't really want to have an abortion. I'm scared.' The defiance melted away and Caroline reverted to being a schoolgirl, crying on her mother's shoulder.

Frank sat down on the settee, his face quite grey at the unpleasantness of the earlier confrontation. Gradually recovering his composure, he said, 'Janet, Caroline - if there's any chance of this working, there's got to be some ground rules - I'm not prepared to keep lying. So there'll be no flannel about who the mother is. And what's more, Caroline, if you hold on to your job, you can pay for the baby's upkeep.'

The telephone rang, cutting into the lecture, which no-one was really taking in. Julie, only too happy to escape for a moment, answered it.

'It's Linda - wants to make sure you're coming.'

'Oh, Barry and Linda. I can't face it.' Janet said tearfully, still with an arm round her daughter. 'Barry is the last person I need right now.'

'Tell Linda we'll be there in an hour,' Frank interrupted. 'We've got to tell them,' he told Janet. 'Let's get it over and done with as soon as possible.'

Julie relayed the message and replaced the telephone. Frank turned to her. 'Julie, the kids will be home after tea at their friends' house. Could you drop Caroline back at the station, if she decides to go back to town, tonight?' Julie meekly nodded agreement, unused to this authoritative side of her brother. 'You will be all right, won't you, Caroline?'

She nodded. 'It'll be good to talk to Julie.'

'Right. And, Caroline, make sure you report to the doctor, and come back next weekend and let us know how you get on?' He turned to Janet. 'I know you're not looking forward to this, love, but we can put up with Barry's snide comments. Linda's looking forward to seeing you. Why don't you put some makeup on and then we'll go.'

Janet blew her nose and obediently disappeared from the room.

Her resilient good humour had stood her in good stead. When she returned soon after, ready to go, she looked almost her old self. Julie followed her and Frank to the front door, and waited, feeling as if she were the hostess watching her guests depart.

'It's been a nightmare - this last week,' Janet said. 'Now I think it's going to be all right. It's been good to talk to you, Julie, and thank you for everything you've said, today.'

She paused at the door.

'Oh, I haven't got any chocs or anything!'

'This'll be fine,' said Frank, returning to grab Julie's bottle of wine from the hall table.

'Love to Linda,' Julie called after them.

'She just bounces back, doesn't she,' marvelled Caroline. 'Chocolates! Wine! The vital issues of the day. Am I going to turn out like that?'

Julie raised one eyebrow in a silent, sceptical response, and turning to the girl, added in a stern voice, 'Let's go and sit down. I've got a few things to say to you!'

Chapter 3: Macho Man

(Monday evening)

The invitation from Barry and Linda was not for a full scale evening meal.

'Come over and have drinks and a snack with us,' Linda had said. 'I'd love a bit of a chat.' That had been three or four weeks ago before their own crisis had blown up, and Janet now remembered the note of urgency in Linda's voice when she had invited them.

The Ford Escort drew up outside the small semi-detached house, the sunshine gleaming on the leadlight windows. Busy lizzies were spilling out of hanging baskets at the front door.

'Well, here we go,' said Frank. The revelation of their daughter's predicament was not going to be pleasant.

'I hope Barry's not in one of his moods,' said Janet.

She got out of the car, straightening her pleated skirt. Frank put an arm round her shoulder, and together they walked up the path.

Linda came to the doorway. 'Hallo, you two. I began to think you weren't coming.' Despite this statement, she didn't appear to be completely ready. Her face, fringed by a smooth, brown bob, was pink and she hadn't yet removed her PVC apron. Janet thought that though Linda was in her late twenties, she always looked like a young girl, playing at being a hostess, and trying hard to do the correct things.

'Yes, sorry we're late,' she said. She hugged her sister-in-law, and followed her into the house. In the living room, Linda had laid out a buffet supper and Barry was sitting with his feet on a coffee table, a glass in hand. He got up to greet the family with some reluctance, as if he was engaged in matters of importance. Janet suppressed her irritation.

Frank proffered the bottle of wine to his brother, and once again, Janet found herself seething at her brother-in-law's ungracious retort.

'Thanks, I've got a beer here. I'm sure Linda will find a use for it in a stew or something.'

Linda blushed and seized the wine saying, 'That looks lovely, Frank. Do you want me to open it? I've already got some white wine - Liebfraumilch - chilled.'

Poor Linda, Janet thought; she was always being embarrassed by Barry's rudeness.

'I'll join Barry in a beer, thanks Lindy - I expect Janet would like the white wine, wouldn't you, love,' said Frank. Janet smiled at him. Always trying to be diplomatic. How could Barry have turned out so different?

'I'd love a glass of white,' she said. 'And after the day we've had, a glass of wine is just what I need.' She sat down in an armchair. 'I'll tell you all about it in a minute. That's what made us a bit late.'

Linda placed the red wine on the sideboard and disappeared into the kitchen. She returned without her apron, clutching a bottle of Liebfraumilch. She poured out wine for two, her eyes on Janet's face. 'What's happened?'

'We've had a few problems - as a matter of fact, we almost didn't come - firstly, Julie's staying with us for a few days - she's had a tiff with her boyfriend.'

She took a sip from her glass.

'Oh well, that's par for the course - I've lost count of Julie's boyfriends,' said Barry, adding with a sneer, 'I'm surprised she can even recognise their faces. I should think they work on a 'hot bed' system.'

He's worse than ever, Janet thought. Frank turned away in angry disgust and it was left to her to reply. Though she lacked confidence in some situations, she was not intimidated by Barry, whereas her sister-in-law seemed to shrink into herself in the face of his bullying.

'You're quite wrong, Barry,' she said. 'It's true that Julie's had a lot of boyfriends - she just hasn't found the right man yet. That doesn't make her promiscuous.'

But Barry would not be deflected. 'If you want my opinion, she's damn lucky not to have ended up with a bun in the oven, by now.'

Janet got up. This was not the moment to impart their news. In any case, first she wanted to catch Linda on her own; she knew that Linda had some problem she was desperate to tell her. 'Can I help you with the food?' she asked Linda.

Linda looked relieved. 'There are a few more things to bring in.'

'I thought you'd done everything,' exclaimed Barry. 'Goodness, you've spent enough time in the kitchen. No wonder you women can't handle more than one job at a time. Industry would fold up if it was all left to you girls, eh, Frank?'

Why on earth didn't Linda stand up for herself, Janet thought. She always seemed vulnerable, but today, all the spirit seemed to have been knocked out of her. It was left to Janet to defend her. 'But Linda does have a job, Barry, doesn't she?'

'Well, that's exactly my point - then she comes home and complains she can't manage to produce a reasonable meal in the evening. I mean look at this stuff - Quiche Lorraine - sounds posh, but it's just a cheese and bacon flan. And a bit of rabbit food. What sort of food is that for company?'

Frank started to speak. Janet knew how he hated to see Barry picking on Linda, and now he could only divert his brother from his unpleasantness by introducing their own bombshell.

'Forget the food, you two. Janet and I have something to tell you. It's going to come as a bit of a shock to you both.'

He paused a little, to let the words sink in. In that brief moment, Barry intervened.

'My God, you're not divorcing, are you?'

For a moment they almost laughed.

'No, of course not.'

'Well, what is it then?'

'It's about Caroline. And it's serious.'

Linda, her face concerned, said, 'She's not ill, Frank, is she?'

'No, not ill, Linda. But unfortunately, she's got herself pregnant.'

At Frank's abrupt statement, Linda gripped the arms of the chair in which she sat, so that her knuckles gleamed white. Then the hands relaxed, but still her face had lost all its colour.

'The stupid little fool,' exclaimed Barry. 'How far is she? Can she still get rid of it?'

An involuntary sob made them all turn to Linda. Barry's words had affected her more than Janet would have expected. As they stared at her, she jumped up, her hand to her face, and ran from the room. Janet raised her eyebrows to her husband and hurried after her sister-in-law. She found Linda in the kitchen, tears running down her face. Janet put her arms round her.

'It's just not fair,' Linda blurted out between sobs. 'We've been trying for five years. How can he talk so easily of getting rid of it? Why does it always happen to girls who don't want them? I'd give anything for a baby now, so why did it happen when I didn't want one... ?' her voice tailed off.

Janet stared at her.

'What do you mean?'

'I've never told you. I did get pregnant ...'

'What, before you knew Barry?'

'No, it was Barry's.'

'You were pregnant before you and Barry got married?'

Linda bit her lips and nodded silently.

'Why didn't you tell me? Maybe I could have helped.'

'I didn't want to tell anyone. I don't know why I'm talking about it now. Except that it's been on my mind so much recently. I've been quite desperate.'

She took a pair of oven gloves from a drawer and turned again to Janet. 'You can't imagine what it's like. I have to avoid mothers with babies and pregnant women. I just can't bear to talk to them.'

Her lips trembled as she spoke. 'And every time we meet new people, it's always, "Have you got any children?" That's the first thing they ask. And when you say "No," they look at you as if there's something wrong with you. Well, there is. But not what they think.'

Pulling on the gloves, she drew a tray of vol-au-vents from the oven, and placed them on the Formica top. 'They say things like, "Plenty of time to get in all the gadgets when you've got your family." They sort of imply that we're being selfish. Just because I like to keep the house nice. But how can I tell them? I'm not just going to come out with it whenever I meet someone. I'm not going to walk up to them and say, "We're failures, Barry and me. We can't have children."'

Janet started to speak, but stopped as Linda carried on.

'I wanted to talk to you about it. But you've got your nice family. You just wouldn't know how it feels. Sometimes I feel as if I'm part of another race.'

'I always thought you wanted children. I just didn't like to ask.'

Tears trickled down Linda's face, and she blew her nose into a square of kitchen roll.

Janet walked into the living room, collected the Liebfraumilch and poured them both another drink. The men were absorbed in the television and ignored her. Returning to the kitchen with full glasses, she said, 'They've got the cricket on. There's no rush.'

Linda sniffed and took a sip. 'I suppose we should toast the baby,' she said, and clinked her glass against Janet's. 'To Caroline's baby.' Another tear ran down her cheek.

Janet mumbled the words, which seemed quite inappropriate at that moment. She went on, 'If you don't mind my asking, what happened to the baby you were expecting? What went wrong?'

'I didn't have an abortion, if that's what you're thinking. I wanted the baby, and I wanted to marry Barry. I loved him. I still do.'

Goodness knows why, Janet thought, managing not to voice the words.

Linda took some plates from the cupboard and cleared a space for them. 'Barry was quite chuffed at the idea that I was pregnant. He kept saying there must be quite a few little Stantons dotted around the Home Counties. I didn't think that was very funny.'

'I should think not,' said Janet. What a pig he is, she thought.

'I knew my family would be upset; my Dad thought Barry was too old for me and he never really liked him.' She swallowed some more wine. 'But I was quite sure. We arranged everything very quickly - do you remember?'

Janet nodded without interrupting.

'We said we wanted a small quiet wedding. It was quite nice really. If only I hadn't felt so guilty about wearing a white dress.'

'You looked lovely.'

'We'd only been married for a month when I miscarried. I never even knew if it was a boy or a girl.' She wiped her eyes. 'It would have been seven by now. At school and everything.'

Janet said nothing, fighting to hold back her own tears, and concentrated on arranging the hot vol-au-vents on one of the plates.

Linda stared for a moment out of the open window. In the silence, they heard the sound of a cricket bat hitting a ball in a neighbouring garden.

'Look the sun's still shining. I've really spoilt this evening for you, haven't I?'

'Don't be silly,' Janet replied. 'It'll do you good to talk.'

'Barry was furious about the miscarriage. And I felt such a failure. I'd got used to the idea and I'd started to look forward to it. I never realised I'd be so disappointed - and so guilty too. It felt like some sort of punishment. I'm sure Caroline would feel the same way if she got rid of her baby. You won't let her, will you?'

Linda listened while Janet explained their plans. All the while, her hands functioned as if they had a life of their own, placing the food in decorative patterns and cutting a pizza into neat slices.

'Thank goodness she's got you, Janet - both of you. You're so understanding. That's why I wanted to tell you about the tests.'

'Tests?'

'Yes. I got a bit desperate recently and I arranged ...'

A shout came from the living room. 'Well, are we going to eat, or aren't we?'

'Oh dear. I'll tell you about it a bit later. Let's take the stuff in and join them.'

Armed with the plates of food, the two women returned to the living room.

Glancing at Linda's flushed face, Barry said, 'What's up with you? Waterworks again?'

Linda bit her lip, and turned away, and the family started to help themselves to snacks from the table. Despite Barry's criticisms, the quiche and pizza were attractively presented, set against the greens and reds of the salads, and the aroma of the freshly baked mushroom vol-au-vents was enticing. Janet, who had not eaten much lunch, took a portion of everything and tucked in with enthusiasm.

'Have you got any left over meat in the fridge?' asked Barry, 'I feel like a cold beef sandwich.'

'For heaven's sake sit down,' Frank boomed out. 'We came here to talk to you both, not to hear you carping about what's on the menu.' He added, turning to Linda with a smile, 'It's all delicious, Lindy - a really nice spread.'

Janet saw that Barry's face had taken on a dull flush. He was still susceptible to a rebuke from his older brother. To cover his embarrassment, he turned to Linda and said, 'Have you heard what these two suckers have decided to do? Frank's just been telling me. You know what I'd do if it were left to me. I'd tell her where to go - and take her little bundle of joy with her.'

Janet said nothing. She couldn't see the point. She wondered if Barry had made a study of being obnoxious. She let Frank speak on behalf of both of them, and he said more gently than was perhaps justified, 'I know you don't really mean that, Barry. I'm sure if you were in our situation you'd do what you could to help.'

Barry put down the mushroom vol-au-vent he was holding and, with a sideways glance at Linda, said, 'In your situation? Parents of three strapping children. Fertility streaming out of every pore. Well, since it seems that either I'm firing blanks, or Madam's as barren as the Gobi Desert, we're not likely to find out, are we?'

For the second time, Linda got up. She turned to Frank. Through clenched teeth she told him, 'Help yourself to anything you want, Frank. There's fruit salad and ice-cream in the fridge. Barry will show you where it is. I'm going for a walk.'

'I'll come too,' said Janet, and she gave Frank a pointed look that meant - he's your brother - give him a good talking-to.

'The worm's turned,' muttered Barry.

'Whatever's got into you?' Frank said, flicking off the TV, as the women went out of the door. 'Why are you treating Linda like dirt? What's happened between you two?'

'What's happened? I'll tell you what's happened - she's no better than that sister of ours.'

Frank looked at his brother blankly. 'What are you talking about?'

'I mean she's no good. She trapped me into a shotgun marriage - has a miscarriage and now she can't get pregnant. I do the dutiful thing - go for tests and what do they tell me? - I'm sub-fertile - so how come she was pregnant in the first place?'

For a moment there was silence. Frank lifted his glass and swallowed a mouthful of beer.

'That's a blow, Barry.' He paused. 'I don't know what we'd do without our kids.'

A faint shout of 'Howzat?' came from the cricket match in the garden next door. It took Frank back to a time when family life seemed uncomplicated.

'Do you remember when Dad taught us to play cricket?' he said.

Barry smiled slightly. 'We used to play in the garden, didn't we? And at the seaside. Even Mum was a fair bat.'

'They were good days,' nodded Frank.

'She was always too busy after Julie came,' said Barry, his smile fading.

'Isn't there some treatment they can give you?' Frank said, twisting his glass.

'Treatment. I'm not even sure I want to go on with the marriage.'

Frank was incredulous. 'Barry, you can't be serious. You know full well that Linda's mad about you. She wouldn't have put up with you otherwise. You've been happy, haven't you?'

Barry hesitated, 'I suppose so. But these tests …'

'If Linda said it was your child, then it was! Sub-fertile doesn't mean infertile - maybe you weren't drinking so much then, maybe you were more relaxed - who knows? Of course it was yours. Stop being a bloody fool.'

'Look,' said Barry, suddenly angry, 'It's easy for you to talk. Everything always comes out right for you. You were always the blue-eyed boy. I was second best. Last in line when Julie came along.' He put his empty plate back on the coffee table. 'Then you have the perfect marriage and three kids into the bargain.'

'We're not in competition,' said Frank. 'You're raking all these things up from the past. But it's the present that's rankling, isn't it?'

'You're right it is!' said Barry and put his hands to his face. 'What sort of a man am I if I can't produce a child?'

Frank, moved by this rare moment of vulnerability, rested a hand on his younger brother's shoulder.

'You've got a problem, Barry. Forget the tough, macho image. Share it with Linda. Don't push her out. Maybe treatment will help - you and Linda almost had a child. It'll happen again.'

He paused, then the words slipped out, 'Don't think that everything's always rosy for Janet and me - it's been damn hard work providing the financial back-up for the perfect wife and mother.'

Barry's eyes widened in surprise.

'What's more - Janet's a lovely girl - don't get me wrong, but sometimes her conversation is rather domestic. I had hoped that she might develop other interests, widen her horizons. But now...' He sighed, before continuing.

'And this latest little package - do you really think I want to go through the nappies and the disturbed nights again? I don't. I'm getting too old for that sort of thing. But I've no option - that's what Janet and Caroline want. I've got to support them.'

He put his beer down abruptly, and looked out of the window, as the clang of the gate announced the return of the two women. Turning back to Barry, he said, 'Why don't you try it?'

Janet and Linda came in, their expressions nervous, as if they didn't know quite what to expect. Linda's face was white and tear-stained.

Barry got up and put an awkward arm around her.

'All right, pet?'

'Yes,' she whispered.'

'How about you two girls sitting down while I make some coffee?'

'I don't think we'll stay for coffee, thanks, Barry,' said Janet, sensing a change in the atmosphere and feeling that, as a social occasion, the evening could be written off.

They walked down the path, turning just once to wave to their in-laws, and got into the car.

'Oh Frank,' said Janet, buckling up her seat belt, 'Thank goodness you're not like Barry.

Fancy having a marriage like that. I'm so lucky to have you - and the kids.'

Frank smiled his slow smile.

'You know what,' she added, 'I know what's happened to Caroline is dreadful. And I'm ashamed to say it, but now we've worked it out, I really feel happy.'

Frank released the hand-brake and let in the clutch. The Escort moved forward.

'I'm really looking forward to it. It's going to be wonderful having a little one in the house again, isn't it?'

He pushed the gear lever into second and patted her hand.

'Absolutely wonderful, darling.'

Chapter 4: 1001 Nights

(Tuesday Morning & Evening)

The reconciliation had been rather a subdued affair. Linda slept badly and rose early. When she left for work, her eyes were still red and her face strained. She arrived twenty minutes before the office opened, and took refuge in the ladies' room.

The receptionist, Helena Fresneau, a smart, blonde woman in her forties, was stationed at the mirror. Linda tried to avoid catching Helena's eyes, but the reflection smiled at Linda and greeted her, before returning to her make-up. Linda mumbled a reply and, for a moment, she forgot her misery and wondered what it would be like to be as confident as Helena. She looked at Helena's cream linen suit with a mixture of envy and admiration. It was stylish, but then, she was always stylish in a way that Linda could never aspire to. You could tell her clothes were expensive - how could she possibly afford something like that on an office worker's salary? But then people said she had a relationship with one of the directors. Could that be true?

As if aware of the thoughts and glances directed at her, Helena turned and regarded

Linda with an astute expression that seemed to take in everything.

'You're not yourself, are you? What's up?'

'It's nothing. I'm fine.'

Linda looked at her face in the glass, blotchy patches showing through this morning's hurried application of make-up, then sent a swift glance at Helena. A sympathetic grin met her eyes.

'Now come on. Who are you trying to kid? You've been crying, haven't you?'

'It was just a tiff with Barry - my husband,' said Linda hesitantly.

'You don't want to let them push you about,' said Helena in a surprising almost Cockney accent, which didn't sound at all like her normal reception and telephone voice. 'If he's giving you a hard time, just learn to keep him under your thumb. How long have you been married?

'Nearly seven years,' replied Linda.

The blonde's eyebrows lifted. 'My goodness, you were barely out of the cradle, weren't you?

Linda flushed.

'I was twenty, she said, her voice sounding defensive even to herself.

'Whatever made you rush into marriage? There's more to life than that, surely.'

'I was pregnant,' replied Linda.

'Does that matter to anyone now?'

'Well it mattered to my Dad. He didn't give Barry a lot of choice.'

'So you were two young innocents playing with fire, and you got your fingers burnt?' Helena said, opening her eyes wide to touch up her mascara.

'Well, actually, Barry was thirty. He - he thought I understood about taking precautions,' Linda said, trying to understate Barry's role in her downfall.

'So he got you in the club, and he's been giving you a hard time ever since,' summed up Helena.

'No - no it's not like that - we've been happy.'

'You don't have to lie to me; I know. Men are swines.'

'No, really,' protested Linda, 'it's just that we had some fertility tests recently - we lost that baby - you see - and Barry was disappointed that I couldn't get pregnant again.'

'So you're spending all your time taking your temperature and working out the right time of the month. No wonder he's pissed off with you.'

'But then we found that he was the one with the problem. And it's been dreadful ever since.'

'I can imagine,' Helena interrupted. 'And you know what. Next thing, he'll go looking for some other nice, naïve, young girl to prove what a man he is.' She carefully applied her lipstick with a brush. 'Maybe *you* should find yourself a boyfriend.'

'I couldn't. I wouldn't want to,' said Linda, shocked.

'Well, he's taking you for granted. I'll bet he's the only man you've ever had. He thinks he can treat you like a worm and you'll put up with it.' She took out a handbag spray and aimed it in the general direction of her neck and her wrists. The scent drifted through the air, making Linda think of exotic evenings in Mediterranean lands. 'You've got to use a bit of psychology, Linda. Keep him interested. Make him jealous. You'll have him in the palm of your hand in no time.'

'I wouldn't know how to,' mumbled Linda.

'Get a life. Go out with friends. Go to the cinema. He probably won't believe that's what you're doing. They never do when you're telling the truth,' said the blonde. 'Then if he thinks someone else fancies you, he'll wonder what he's missing.'

'But where would I go? All my friends are married. And I have to cook in the evenings,' Linda protested.

'You really do lead a sheltered life, don't you?' said Helena, shaking her head. 'You can't run your life round Barry's tea.'

She turned again to the mirror and flicked one or two blonde curls with a small comb.

'I'll tell you what,' she exclaimed, suddenly inspired. 'Come and join me for a coffee and a sandwich tonight.' She took an envelope from her bag and scribbled down her address. 'Do you know where this is? It's only a couple of streets from here.'

'I'm not sure if I should,' said Linda, aware, even as she said it, that she would not be able to resist the invitation.

That evening, when Barry arrived home and sat himself in an armchair with a beer, she walked in with a ham salad and a trifle on a tray, and placed it in front of him.

'I'm going out to meet a friend,' she told him, to his astonishment. 'I won't be back till late.'

Glancing around the room to check that everything had been left tidy, she spotted the bottle of red wine on the sideboard where she had placed it the previous day. She hesitated, wondering if it would be ungrateful to dispense with Janet and Frank's gift. But something had changed. A new Linda was shedding some of the inhibitions of the old.

'I'll take this with me,' she said to Barry, as she departed.

She was used to the tube journey which she took every morning to work. Now, instead of strap hanging commuters, it was filled with young people going out for the evening. Most of them seemed to be dressed in the conventional uniform of baggy jeans, in spite of the warm weather. Looking at herself with new eyes, Linda felt rather prim and old fashioned in her Laura Ashley dress.

Once she had arrived, it didn't take long to find Helena's address. When she saw the luxurious apartment block in which Helena lived, she almost turned and ran in the opposite direction. But her curiosity got the better of her. She went past the uniformed commissionaire, announced her presence through a speaker and took the lift to the second floor.

Helena was waiting for her at the door. She wore some well tailored white trousers, which enhanced her slim figure, and a cashmere sweater. But without make-up it was possible to see the lines around her eyes that had not been so obvious before. Whereas, at her post in reception she could pass for thirty, now she looked nearer to her actual age.

The room was welcoming, and decorated with taste. Heavy brocade curtains framed the window, through which the late sunshine now streamed. A photograph of a boy in his late teens sat in pride of place on a mahogany bureau.

'I've brought some wine,' said Linda feeling awkward. She handed Helena the bottle.

'That was a nice thought,' smiled the hostess. 'I won't open it just now. Sit yourself down, Linda, and make yourself comfortable. I've poured us a Martini - do you like Martini?'

'Mm,' Linda replied. She sank back onto the cushions of the leather sofa and sipped the drink. It was a little dry for her, and well laced with gin, but after a few mouthfuls she felt false courage beginning to seep into her bloodstream.

Helena had laid out a buffet of sandwiches and other finger food. Linda picked up a delicately-made triangular sandwich and popped it into her mouth.

'Ooh, smoked salmon, lovely. How comfortable it is here.'

'I'm good at making other people comfortable, Linda,' said the older woman. 'You could say that's one of my few talents. That and passable looks. And they're going a bit now, so I have to make sure I don't lose my other talents. I wouldn't have my flat or my job if I didn't keep Lawrence happy and then I wouldn't be able to keep my boy at college either.'

'Your boy?' stammered Linda.

'Yes, that's his picture. I also got knocked up when I was in my twenties. *That* bastard disappeared like greased lightning when I told him I was in the club. I tried a bottle of gin and a hot bath and all that. Not a very nice experience - I really prefer gin as a short drink. None of it worked and I had no spare cash. So I just muddled through. I swore I'd never let a man get the upper hand again. Though Lawrence is a kind bloke.'

'Yes, he seems very nice,' Linda said, then blushed at her slip, for she was not sure she was supposed to know the identity of Helena's lover.

But Helena gave a good-natured chuckle. 'Everyone knows, don't they, except poor Gwen. That sad sack of a wife. Yes, he's a good bloke, but I don't take things for granted. He never quite knows what's coming next, whether it's food, wine, sex or anything.'

Linda's mouth dropped open a little.

'I keep him interested and I keep him coming back for more. Just like that sheikh's wife in the Arabian nights. A different story every night. I'm nothing more than a high class pro really. Except that I can't help loving the old sod too, so I hope I can keep the magic going.' A shadow crossed her face for a moment then she grinned. 'Come and have a look at the Boudoir.'

Linda followed her into a room with a thick Persian carpet on the floor. A king size bed was made up with pastel satin sheets. Helena switched on a light which threw a glow of scarlet into the room. Another switch brought on a stereo. Oriental music played.

'I do like the exotic,' commented Helena, spraying herself and Linda liberally with a musky, heady perfume, 'but I've got all sorts of music.'

She opened a drawer revealing rows and rows of cassettes. 'Here's Ravel's Bolero. I heard it in some film with Bo Derek. Before your time, dear; it must have been ten years ago. Used to turn her on. Does the same for me. I liked it even before Torvill and Dean. Weren't they fabulous at the Olympics?' Linda didn't manage to get in an answer, before she took out another tape. 'I like The Stripper too.'

'Are they all your clothes in that cupboard?' asked Linda, looking agog at the long, full width wardrobe, which was half open. Helena slid the mirrored door back to reveal numerous outfits filling the space. Silk underwear of black and purple and scarlet hung cheek by jowl with demure long-sleeved nighties of alabaster and delicate rose-petal pink.

'I have been known to feel bridal,' commented Helena. 'I'm quite a sentimental soul really. Sometimes I get maudlin when I'm on my own. He doesn't come every night of course. It's nice to have some company.'

She led Linda into an ensuite bathroom.

'This is a bit of a pig to clean,' she said, indicating an olive sunken bath. 'Still, we like to have a bath or shower together. Lawrence says it reminds him of rugby - vive le difference, I say. Well, enough of this nonsense. Let's go and have some more sandwiches and a nice cup of coffee, and I'll tell you all about my boy.'

As she described her son in glowing terms, she could have been any middle aged mother full of maternal pride.

'She's no different to Janet,' thought Linda and felt again that stab of sorrow that she herself could not share in this particular joy.

There was so much to talk about that it came as a surprise to Linda when she realised it was already ten-thirty. Helena pressed Linda to take a taxi home.

'Spoil yourself sometimes, dear, if he won't. We all deserve a little cosseting. But if you get him sorted out, he'll be the one to do the pampering. You take notice of what I say. Forget about getting pregnant for a bit. Maybe you will have a baby, maybe you won't. Have some fun in the meantime - both of you.'

Linda got out of the cab carrying a Gucci carrier bag.

'Have a little treat on me,' Helena had said, pushing it into her hand.

The house was in darkness. Linda turned on the light and smiled. She was aware that the alcohol was making her feel quite unlike her normal self. She went to the stack system, put on a cassette of 'Ravel's Bolero' and turned the volume up loud. She noticed with disapproval the empty beer can in the lounge and the unwashed plates in the kitchen, but chose to ignore them.

'When I've got him eating out of my hand, like Helena said, things'll be different,' she told herself, stripping off her clothes and leaving them where they fell on the living room floor.

She opened the carrier bag and donned the wisps of black lace contained within, with shaking hands, careful not to snag the flimsy material. Black fishnet stockings and a red suspender belt completed the effect. She teetered up the stairs in her high heels and opened the bedroom door, turning on the dimmer switch, so that the pink shaded lights brought a soft glow to the room. The music followed her, its insistent repetitious melody increasing in volume and urgency. Linda waited at the foot of the bed, her hands on her hips, as her husband's breathing became irregular and he made small wakeful grunts. As Ravel's Bolero reached an excited crescendo, Barry opened his eyes.

Chapter 5: Behind Net Curtains

(Wednesday morning and evening)

At Reception, the telephone rang. Helena picked it up, her other hand occupied in waving to Linda, whose brilliant smile and pink cheeks told her all she needed to know about the previous night.

Still smiling, she chanted in her front of house voice, 'Chapman and Hillborough.'

'Helena, it's me.'

Helena dropped the sing-song mode. 'What do you want, Justin?'

'I need to see you. I wondered if you'd drop over tonight, Sis.'

Helena winced at the word 'Sis'.

'I wish you wouldn't call me at work. I don't like having personal calls. People are passing through all the time.'

'Keep your hair on, Sis.'

'What is it anyway? Money?'

She'd been bailing him out as long as she could remember, and it didn't make for an easy relationship.

'What do you take me for?' Justin said, interrupting her thoughts.

'If it's money you're after, Justin, you can just forget it,' Helena said. She didn't want to be harsh, but she wasn't going to be taken for a ride again.

'I want to talk to you about Ma.'

He always knew which buttons to press. Helena felt her heart lurch. 'Is she all right?'

'I'll tell you all about it tonight.'

Helena's brain kicked into gear again.

'You conned me last time you brought Mum into the equation.'

'If you come tonight, I'll explain about that...'

'You told me that the home had asked for four hundred pounds for a special course of drugs. You told me you'd paid them. And I was stupid enough to believe you. When I went to see them, they didn't know anything about it. Didn't even have your number.'

'It's just one nurse, see. She does everything for Ma, and I've been giving her cash on the QT. It's no good talking to the officials. They'll just give you a load of bull.'

'But why would you need to pay out extra money?'

'She needs someone to keep an eye on her. Otherwise ...'

'Otherwise what?'

'Otherwise it could be nasty. Just come tonight. I can't explain on the phone.'

There were all sorts of things that could be going on at the home. Sometimes you heard about bullying at these places. Helena felt her resolve slip.

'All right. I'll come.'

'See you then, Sis - say about seven.'

'That's too early. I won't have time to eat. It'll have to be nearer eight thirty.'

He didn't ask her to come for a meal, just grumbled, 'Oh well, just make it as early as you can.'

'OK,' she agreed, her mind now full of the potential problems at the home.

During the day she continued to speculate on the possibilities. She couldn't bear to think of her elderly mother being bullied, whether it was by the staff or other patients. Or maybe drugged so that she was nothing more than a vegetable, though she heard this sort of thing went on at these old people's homes, when the patients were difficult.

Helena knew she wasn't the best of daughters. It upset her to see that her mother's mind had gone and she had ceased to be the person Helena remembered; most times she blotted it from her mind. But she did the best she could. She made sure she found the cash for a private nursing home, and that was on top of John's boarding school fees - she wanted her family to have the best of everything.

Should she look out for somewhere else for Mum, she wondered. Closer perhaps, so she could call in more often. It wouldn't be so bad if Justin pulled his weight. She'd thought things might improve when he got married. After all, his beloved Andrea might have been modelled on one of the Stepford Wives. She was always immaculate and seemed to spend her entire life cooking, and dusting dinky ornaments. If anyone could have made him respectable, she could. For a while it seemed to have worked and, for quite a long time, there hadn't been any requests for handouts. Then she started getting the occasional phone-call with a plea for a bit extra. Apart from that, she didn't get to see either of them very often and that suited her fine. She and Andrea hadn't clicked at all - no surprise there - she just wasn't Helena's cup of tea.

But, to give him his due, Justin had sounded genuinely concerned on the telephone. She felt a brief glow of affection for him, pleased that he still cared about the old girl in spite of her present state.

That night, she ate a solitary meal of steak and vegetables and debated whether to open the wine that Linda had left the previous day. She picked up the bottle - just a bog-standard supermarket red. Someone had drawn a funny little doodle on it which, at first sight, looked part of the label. Could it have been Linda? No there was an initial 'J'. 'J' for - who knows? She might as well take it to Justin; He'd never notice and it would be a gesture of good will.

She placed the bottle next to the car keys and got ready to go.

Arriving at Justin's pleasant semi shortly after eight o'clock, she collected the wine from the back of the car and walked towards the door which was framed by pink clematis blossom. In the evening sunshine, the net curtains looked less crisp and white than usual.

She rang the chiming bell which had always irritated, as it seemed a confirmation of all Andrea's suburban habits.

Justin came to the door and opened it a crack.

'Let me in, Justin. Stop mucking about.'

He opened the door and pulled her in. She looked at his face. It was thin and dark with strain.

'Tell me about Mum, Justin. What's been going on?'

He opened the kitchen door.

'You'd better come in here. We've got the decorators in, in the other room.'

Helena followed him into the kitchen and put the wine down on the work-surface. Despite the pigtail, a male fashion which she didn't like at all, Justin was as good looking as ever. That blue-black hair, and surprisingly blue eyes. You had to be very careful not to give in to him, just because of his looks. He was always wheedling things out of her when he was a little boy and Mum had spoiled him rotten too. And now her John was getting to look like him. She'd better keep an eye on him and make sure he didn't go the same way.

'Well?'

'Look, I'll get you a drink. Let me explain what's happened.'

Helena watched as he poured a couple of miserly Martinis into two beakers and topped them up with lemonade. Of the fancy crystal glassware that Andrea was so proud of, there was no sign.

She sat down on the only kitchen stool.

'There's this nurse. She collared me the last time I went there. Said she could keep Ma out of trouble.'

'Which one was it? That small one with the dark hair, what's her name? Doreen? She's a nice girl.'

'Yeah, that might have been her.'

'Or was it Martine, the blood-nut?'

'What does it matter? Just listen, will you?'

'Well, whoever she is, I'd like to talk to her about all this. We pay enough. We shouldn't have to fork out extra. And what kind of trouble is it?'

'Don't worry about it. Just give me some money and I'll get it sorted.'

There was something wrong with his story. Now she was here, the old doubts started up again. She glanced out of the window. The sky was getting darker. She shivered involuntarily.

'Why don't you put the light on, Justin?'

'The bulb's gone. I forgot to get a spare.'

The place looked so unkempt. Helena ran a finger over the kitchen work surface and it was grubby.

'Where's Andrea?' she asked.

'Never mind Andrea. We've had a little tiff, and she's gone home to Mum. She'll be back. She'll soon start missing me,' he added, a supercilious smile playing on his lips. Helena was familiar with that look, but tonight it seemed a bit forced.

'What did you fight about? I didn't think Andrea was the argumentative type.'

'She bought a pricey three piece suite and got us into the red. Look, what does it matter?'

He shouldn't have said that, Helena thought, because at that moment she knew.

'Why are you decorating if you're so short of cash?' she asked.

'I didn't know until today, did I?' He took out a handkerchief and wiped his forehead.

'Where's this posh suite then. Let's have a look at it,' said Helena getting up from the stool.

'Eh? Well, we haven't got it yet.'

'Well, why don't you just cancel it?'

'Why all the questions?' said Justin, his face getting dark and sulky. He stood up himself and put his hand on her arm. 'Are you going to give me some cash or aren't you?'

'Stop lying to me, Justin. There is no problem at the home, is there? Mum's OK, isn't she?'

'What are you talking about? What do you take me for?'

Helena ignored the questions. Putting aside Justin's restraining hand, she walked out of the kitchen. She opened the lounge door and peered in.

She let out a gasp. 'Oh my Gawd. Whatever's happened?' The room was completely empty of furniture, carpets and furnishings, devoid of all the knickknacks and well known prints that Andrea so liked. Of decorators, or their accoutrements, there was no sign.

Justin followed her into the bare room.

'Where is everything, Justin?' Helena gasped.

His face was white now. She felt a moment of pity for him, in spite of everything.

'You've got to help me, Sis. I'll tell you the truth. You're bound to find out. Andrea's taken everything. Well at least, what she hasn't taken herself, she's either sold or the bailiffs have taken.'

'Bailiffs?' echoed Helena.

'Look, Sis, I don't know how to tell you this, but Andrea's a compulsive gambler. She has been for years. Now we're wiped out. We're in debt up to our eyeballs. She's overdrawn every joint account we've got. She's hocked things - the good things, that is. She left all that cheap tat around so it wasn't noticeable that the good stuff was going.'

'Couldn't you stop her?' asked Helena, amazed at this unknown side of her sister-in-law.

'Stop her - I didn't even realise until a couple of months ago. She fooled me completely - well you can understand that - she fooled you too, didn't she?'

'Yes,' admitted Helena.

'She owed so much, she couldn't handle it - that's when she told me. I couldn't believe it. If there was a flutter going, she was in on it.'

'Well, who'd have believed she had it in her,' marvelled Helena. 'Isn't there anything left?'

Without answering, Justin led her upstairs to the bedroom.

The camp bed from the loft had pride of place in the otherwise empty room. Helena suddenly noticed the net curtains, hanging drab and grey on the windows. Andrea would never have allowed them to stay up in that state. And yet, and yet, it seemed she had other things on her mind.

Brother and sister sat down side by side on the bed.

'It started with small stuff, horse racing on TV, greyhound racing - that sort of thing.'

Helena tried to imagine Andrea at the greyhound track and failed.

'Then there were the nights out at the Casino - one or two evenings a week - said she was at evening class. But the real trouble came when she started with stocks and shares. Investment she called it - she was on the phone to the stockbroker day in, day out, watching the shares rise on teletext, "sell" one day, "buy" the next. While the stock market was rising, that was OK; she was making money and having fun at the same time. The stakes were getting higher and higher. It was like a giant crap game.'

'Then what happened?' asked Helena, fascinated.

'Black Monday.'

'What's that?'

'You must have read about it. Eighteen months ago - October 1987 - the Stock Market crash. Don't you remember?'

Helena shook her head. She didn't get involved with stocks and shares.

'Take my word for it. It was bad. And Andrea couldn't believe the bubble had burst. She went on buying, selling like there was no tomorrow, but it was all wrong. Each time the account ended she was out of pocket and it's all been downhill from then onwards. It was back to the Casino, staking big money to try to get back to Square One. But it didn't work. The only thing we've got left is the house and she couldn't get at that without my signature.'

'You say she's gone home now.'

'Yeah. Once I wouldn't agree to sign away the house, she left - she went back to her parents - heaven help them - took a few bits and pieces, and the bailiffs took the rest. The electricity's off. The phone's off.'

'I can't believe this, Justin - it's the most terrible thing I've ever heard,' said Helena, filled with unusual sympathy for her brother. 'But I don't know if I can help. How much do you need?'

'Helena, I wouldn't ask you, but I'm still being chased by people for these debts of hers. If you could see your way clear to letting me have a couple of grand - just to tide me over - that would get me out of trouble - just until I've got myself sorted out.'

Helena hesitated. 'A couple of thousand pounds, Justin - that's a lot of money.'

'Not to you surely, Sis. I've seen that Golf you drive. You must be raking it in.'

'Look, Justin, it's true I've got a good job. But the car's not in my name. And I'm still shelling out for John, and for Mum too, don't forget. I couldn't give you more than a thousand.'

Justin's lips quivered. His blue eyes bore into her.

'Please, Helena. I'm in real trouble.'

'A thousand is all I can do, Justin. That's about as much as I can cope with.'

His face distorted with disappointed fury.

'You self satisfied bitch,' he snarled. 'Cope with - you're not coping with anything. You've packed Ma into a home, and your precious bastard's miles away, so you don't have to think about either of them. As for your *good job* - you call that a job? You get money for jam - waggling your arse to impress a lot of dirty old men. Shacked up with the dirtiest of the lot. Your face plastered with makeup like Polyfilla. Well, make the most of it, you stupid tart. When your old man has a heart attack, you'll be back on the street where you belong.'

Helena felt the colour drain from her face. Her hands shook, as she picked up her bag. 'I'm sorry for your trouble, Justin. I would have tried to help you, but I won't be spoken to like that. Don't ring. Don't contact me. I don't want to see you again.'

'Look, Sis,' whined Justin. 'Don't take umbrage. I was only joking.'

'Not my idea of a joke,' said Helena, biting her lips to stop the tears. 'I mean what I say - stay out of my life.'

She walked out of the bedroom, feeling her way down the stairs in almost total darkness.

The 'ding-dong' of the chiming bell startled her. She heard Justin's voice whisper hoarsely, 'Don't open it.' She arrived in the hall and hesitated. Then the heavy thump of a shoulder hitting the door replaced the musical box tinkle and, even as she stood there, the latch gave way and the door flew open.

The silhouette of the intruder was framed in the doorway, his face shadowed, his tall powerful frame blotting out the street lighting.

'Justin Fresneau?' came a smooth voice with a trace of a European accent.

'He's not in,' she lied, trying to stop her voice shaking.

Just behind her own car, in the quiet road, she could see the dark shape of another vehicle, a long car like a Mercedes and the outline of other figures inside it.

The man extended his arm and took hold of her shoulder. She felt the grip of hard fingers. With his other hand, he took out a lighter and flicked it on and drew it up to her face. The light glinted on a large square ring on one of his fingers, and she felt the heat of the flame next to her cheek. She looked up at him and saw a sallow thin face with dark eyes and as she stared, reluctantly transfixed, like the prey of a snake, his pupils contracted to needle points in the sudden light.

'Madame, I would advise you to speak the truth. One would not wish to hurt a beautiful lady, but I have my instructions.' He snapped off the lighter and Helena exhaled in relief. In the darkness, he brought his face even nearer and his fingers tightened. 'I have to collect some money from Mr Justin Fresneau. And, as you see, my companions have come too, in case Mr Fresneau shows reluctance in parting with this money. I regret, Madame, I cannot let you stand in my way.'

The over polite words contrasted with the feel of his hand, almost on her throat.

'What does he owe this money for?' asked Helena, her heart thudding, but her voice in control.

'I regret that Mr Fresneau has incurred debts at a certain club. A gentleman always pays his gambling debts, Madame. That is understood.'

For the first time, he let his hand drop back to his side.

'Look, it's not Mr Fresneau's fault. His wife is the one who built up the debts,' said Helena, though she was sure that her statement would make no difference.

'I regret you are mistaken, Madame. Mr Fresneau has been to the club a great deal. I have met him there myself, on many occasions.'

Of course. How could she have been so stupid as to fall for Justin's story? It was as full of holes as a fishing net and she was the fish who'd nearly got caught, once again. Nevertheless, it only increased the danger of Justin's position.

She had not totally believed him when he said he was in trouble. Now she was confronted with the truth of that statement, at least. For a moment the vision of her brother as a small boy, a boy like her own son John, flashed before her eyes.

'How much money does Mr Fresneau owe this place?' she asked.

'I have been told to collect twelve hundred pounds, Madame,' the man replied.

Helena summoned up all her courage. 'Look, I'm prepared to make you an offer. You can go in there and beat up Mr Fresneau and break up the happy home. But that won't get your money back. Because he hasn't got any. I can see you're a business man. I'm prepared to give you a cheque for a thousand pounds, if you'll call it a day at that.'

The man hesitated.

'We do not normally deal in cheques, Madame, in these circumstances. Mr Fresneau's own cheques have not been honoured.'

Helena stood very erect and looked taller than her five foot six.

'You have my personal guarantee. I wouldn't take the risk of your coming back and hurting him. I'll make the cheque out to cash.' She took her cheque book out of her bag. 'Well, how about it?'

He hesitated, then took the book from her, ignited the lighter once again and glanced down at the cheque book. The thin lips smiled slightly at the name 'Fresneau' and he shrugged in indifferent agreement.

'A thousand pounds, Madame?'

'Yes,' replied Helena in a firm voice.

Her hand shook slightly, as she started writing out the cheque by the glow from the lighter, once again held, like an unspoken threat, near to her flesh, the heat of the small flame almost singeing the hairs on her wrist.

The cheque complete, he snapped out the lighter and turned to go.

'Madame,' he said, pausing and half turning back towards her.

'Yes.'

'Tell Mr Fresneau he is no longer welcome at the club.'

He walked down the pathway to the long black car which waited, looking incongruous in the suburban street. Helena stood alone in the doorway. She glanced back to see her brother's silhouette at the top of the stairs. Then she slammed the door and walked to her car.

The answer-phone light was flashing when she got home. Lawrence's cultured voice was on the tape.

'Sorry you're out, Helena. Gwen has gone away on a WI Conference - she's the main representative. I should have let you know earlier. I would have liked to have seen you tonight.'

His voice was warm and reassuring. Relief brought tears to her eyes. Wiping them away, she telephoned his number.

'Lawrence, I'm so glad to hear your voice. Sorry I was out when you phoned. I had a little domestic problem. Come over as soon as you can, darling. I'll put some champagne on ice and make us a snack.'

She showered quickly, watching the swirling water disappear down the drain and imagining that Justin's unsavoury world was being sucked away along with the bubbles.

Then she busied herself with the preparations for Lawrence's visit. She filled the table with inviting delicacies and found the promised bottle of champagne. Polished glasses glinted on the table and a vase of freesias exuded a light fragrance into the air.

Helena studied her face in the mirror, wiped off most of her make-up and changed into an ivory satin negligee. She combed her hair into a casual style.

'Bridal,' she murmured to herself and sat back to wait for her man.

Chapter 6: Crime and Punishment

(Thursday early evening)

The situation was getting desperate. Justin had paced the floor the whole day. One belligerent creditor had been satisfied, but what about the others?

The trouble was, he couldn't think straight. He had to have a plan of campaign. It wasn't just about money, bankruptcy and all that. Now there were all these characters out to get him. Who knows what they'd do to him if he couldn't pay his gambling debts?

He'd sit down and have a drink. That would relax him and he'd be able to think clearly. There was that bottle of red wine Helena had left behind. It didn't look too bad. No. It was stupidity. The problems would be blotted out for an hour or so, and then he'd be back to square one.

He'd have to go and plead with Andrea. Surely, if she understood the danger he was in, she'd give in. He'd take the wine with him. It would give him a bit of dignity when he walked in on her parents, but he wouldn't hesitate to use it as a weapon, if he had problems en route.

He scoured the half empty wardrobe, shaking his clothes to see if any cash fell out. In one pair of trousers he heard the jingle of coins. The sound led him to the discovery of three pound coins and a fifty pence piece. It was enough at least for a taxi.

With the telephone cut off, he had to undertake the risky walk to the main road. He sneaked along the pavement - not too fast, not too slow - all the while looking for suspicious strangers, threatening shadows. He kept the bottle at his side. He could hardly be accused of carrying an offensive weapon, taking some wine on a visit to his estranged wife and parents-in-law.

He spotted a taxi and hailed it. Ten minutes later, he drew up at the small bungalow which he had visited many times, often with reluctance, in other circumstances.

The chime of the bell was identical to that which Andrea had installed at their home.

Andrea appeared at the door. She had a duster in her hand which looked out of place with the slim black skirt and white blouse she was wearing. She was lightly scented with lavender.

Her face grew tense when she saw her husband, and he felt an involuntary stab of desire for her. She was the antithesis of everything he wanted in a woman, and yet he couldn't help being attracted to her cool and trim good looks.

'What do you want?'

'Just a little social visit. I miss my conjugal rights,' he said, knowing, as the words left his mount, that they would antagonise her, but unable to help himself. He held out the wine, but she ignored the extended hand.

'Don't I get invited in, Doll?' he said. 'Where's the welcome for the old man?'

'I'd rather you didn't come in, Justin. Say what you have to say and go.'

'It's cold out here. I'm in trouble, Andrea.'

She had a soft heart – she'd always relented in the past.

'I'm not sure,' she said, biting her lip. 'My parents …'

He was getting impatient with her dithering. He pushed his way into the hall and, placing the bottle down on the hall table, grabbed hold of her arms and pulled her towards him. The duster dropped from her hand, and her body stiffened in terror, while her nails clawed at his face.

'Bitch,' he said. 'As frigid as ever! Still suffering from rigor mortis. Sex doesn't fit in with your clean-living existence, does it? I bet you'd rather dust the Dresden than have a romp in the hay.'

She was shivering with fear. 'What have you come for, Justin?'

With an effort, he restrained himself, remembering how much he needed her co-operation.

'Look, sorry, Doll. I wouldn't really push myself on you, if you didn't want it.'

She looked unconvinced.

'Well, not now we're apart, anyway.' He looked around. 'Where are the old folk? Are they here?'

'They're upstairs. Just don't touch me, or I'll give them a call.'

She never was a good liar. The house was too quiet. 'They're out, aren't they? Naughty Andrea. Telling porkies.'

She flushed. 'If you must know, they've gone out for the evening, Justin. But I'm expecting someone soon. So you can just tell me what you want.'

Desire surged up in him again.

'You know what I want, Doll.'

Again she recoiled. Again he checked himself.

'Look, now we seem to be splitting up, I want my share of the house. All I want is for you to sign that you're in agreement to the sale. I'll give you your share as soon as the sale goes through.'

'You must think I'm stupid, Justin. Do you think I'd fall for that? When you've gone through every penny we've ever possessed?'

She took a small step back as she spoke and he moved a fraction forward, as if they were carrying out a slow motion dance routine. Justin took a squashed packet of cigarettes from his pocket and lit one. The nicotine steadied him. Aware of all he had to lose, he made an effort to subdue her fearfulness.

'Look, Doll. Why don't you grab a pew and we'll talk this over calmly? How about a fag or a drink?' He picked up the bottle of wine.

She ignored both suggestions. 'Sit down if you must, Justin. Though I don't think there's anything more to say.'

She led the way into the living room and placed herself on the edge of an upright chair, her back to the open door, looking stiff and uncomfortable.

The grandmother clock in the hall chimed a quarter before the hour.

Justin spread himself out in a chintzy armchair, putting the wine down on the low coffee table in front of him and flicking ash into a Venetian glass ashtray.

'All I want is my share of the house. That's reasonable, isn't it?'

'Do you think I'm going to let you gamble away our house as well as everything else? I'm not signing anything without my solicitor present. Half that house is morally mine and I don't believe you'd let me have half the proceeds. If you think I'm coming back to my parents without a penny of my own after eight years of marriage, you're very much mistaken.'

He let her make her little speech, then tried to sound reasonable.

'Look, Doll, the problems I've had are temporary. I had good stock market investments. I've still got hunches. All I need is a bit of cash and a change in the economic climate.'

'Justin, investment means having money in safe places. The bank; the building society. Putting money in risky things isn't investing - it's gambling.'

For a moment she looked at him with an expression that was almost tender. Was she going to relent? But no. It was just a lecture.

'I'd have stood by you if you'd joined Gamblers Anonymous, when I suggested it, when I realised. Maybe we could have worked something out. But you wouldn't face the truth - you won't ever learn. People go out to work to get money. There is no such thing as easy money.'

She'd got to understand. He'd remind her of the good times.

'You're forgetting how great things were a few years ago. Remember the parties we used to go to - and the clubs. Remember the frocks you used to wear. It was the Stock Market problems that spoiled everything.'

'Parties,' she scoffed. 'Excuses for poker games. Yes, I remember getting dressed up for trips to Casinos. I remember the high when you won. I remember how you used to take it out on me when you lost. I lived in dread of those parties. But, even then, I didn't realise you were raiding our accounts to put money in high risk investments. And when we had nothing left, you were betting with money we hadn't got.'

'Well, you don't look too bad on it. We never starved, did we?'

'We never starved because I took on a cleaning job, while you were out gambling. Then when I got the cash, I went straight to the shops and bought food and paid other household expenses.'

He laughed outright at that.

'You! You took a cleaning job. Well, I never thought you had it in you. Scrubbing people's floors. Cleaning other people's loos. Unbelievable! I always thought you'd crept back to the old folks for a bit of cash.'

'I had my pride. I had to be at rock bottom to come back here now. It's not easy to hear, "I told you so."'

'So the parents warned you off, did they?' laughed Justin bitterly.

'They didn't like your family at all, as a matter of fact,' stated Andrea. 'They said you were down-market people with up-market names. They thought that Helena was a slut and you were a scoundrel.'

'Well, well. I never thought they were so astute,' said Justin. 'They really had us sussed out, didn't they? So they didn't think much of poor old Helena, either. Well, I can tell you, she doesn't think much of you, particularly now she knows your reputation.'

'My reputation?' said Andrea colouring.

'Yes, you'll never be able to borrow from any of Helena's rich friends - she thinks you're a compulsive gambler.'

Andrea just stared at him. 'I'm not going to lose a lot of sleep over that.'

Justin sensed he was losing the plot. He mustn't get side-tracked.

'Look, Doll, if we could just come back to my present problems. If we could dispose of the house, the money coming in would sort me out. It's not just the investments that are causing me a headache - I've got some unpleasant types breathing down my neck. I think I might be in for some trouble.'

'Justin - I don't wish any harm to come to you. Goodness knows - I know what it's like to feel afraid of being beaten up,' she added, 'but I am not signing away the house.' The clock in the hall struck seven, and Andrea's eyes turned to her watch. 'And if you don't mind, I'd like you to go now.'

He caught the glance.

'You're waiting for someone.'

'I said I was.'

'You've got some fancy man coming, haven't you? You cow, you don't give a damn about me, because you've got someone else lined up. Some sugar daddy, like my whore of a sister.'

Andrea said nothing. Her eyes showed fear at the recognition of a familiar look in his eyes.

'You've been a naughty girl, haven't you, Doll? You've been a bad wife. You know what happens to naughty girls, Andrea, don't you? They get punished.'

Andrea tried to slide the chair backwards away from him.

He was aroused by her fear and her vulnerability. If he wasn't going to get any cash out of her, then at least he'd enjoy giving her something she wouldn't forget.

'You know what I think, Doll. I think your boyfriend wouldn't like you so much if you had a couple of black eyes. Perhaps you'd be glad to come back to me then and do as you're told.'

'Stay away from me, Justin,' she said in a shaking voice.

They both stood up together. He started towards her. She kicked over the coffee table into his path. The bottle and ashtray slid, undamaged, to the floor, but the table gave his shins a sharp rap which hurt, and he swore.

He started to undo a metal ended belt. She backed away from him, retreating into the hall doorway behind her. He followed, swinging the belt through the air. The clasp caught her cheek a glancing blow, causing blood to run down the side of her face. He felt his own blood pounding through his veins. She screamed and ran the last few yards to the doorway, almost falling to the floor in her panic.

The incongruous sound of the door chimes started, playing their thin musical box melody.

Andrea scrambled to her feet, opened the door and began to weep. 'David,' she said, her voice choked with tears.

The young man who stood there could have been nine or ten years younger than Justin. Tall and thin, he looked like a modern version of 'Mr Chips', his glasses and serious expression contributing to that school-masterly appearance.

'Well, haven't you done well, Doll?' sneered Justin. 'Arnold Schwarzenegger to a tee.'

David looked from one to the other and said, 'Phone the police, Annie.'

'Annie! Is that what your toy boy calls you? What did you pick *her* out for, Professor? If you wanted to learn the ropes, you should have found yourself a real woman. All she can teach you is how to clean loos.'

'Shut up,' David muttered. 'Phone the police,' he repeated to Andrea.

'Not the police,' she pleaded and Justin felt a moment's satisfaction. She still cared about him.

'She thrives on it really,' he said, grabbing her by the hair and pulling her towards him. He kissed her hard on the lips. 'Perhaps you've learned something from that, teacher.'

As Andrea gasped and wrenched herself free, Justin felt a hard blow land on his face and reeled as blood started pouring from his nose.

'Leave her alone,' David gasped, his voice shaking. 'Are you going to get the police, Andrea?'

'Just get him out of here,' she sobbed. 'I don't want to have to see him or have anything to do with him.'

'Did you hear that?' said David, taking Justin by the collar and ushering him to the door. 'Stay away from Andrea. Don't come back here again.'

He shoved Justin out of the house, so that he fell to the ground. The door slammed shut behind him. Struggling to his feet, Justin cursed and aimed one last kick at the door before limping onto the darkening street. He edged along the pavement. He coughed as blood trickled down the back of his throat, and held his hand to his face to try to stem the flow. He could do with a drink, but he didn't even have the bottle of wine.

He wandered in the direction of his home, a home where no-one waited, no-one would welcome him. He tried to think of anyone who might offer him refuge and there was no-one.

Chapter 7: Lavender

(Thursday evening)

'I've never seen you like this before, David,' said Andrea, sitting up, her shoulders taut, in the armchair so recently vacated by her husband. 'I could hardly believe it was you, just now.'

'I was a bit surprised myself,' he admitted.

David knelt on the floor next to her, a pad of cotton wool in his hand. He dabbed at the wound with a gentle hand. Even so, Andrea winced and took a shaky sip from a glass of brandy he had poured for her.

Making a face at the taste, she offered it to him.

'This is horrible. Why don't you have it? You look as if you could do with it as much as me.'

'Rubbish, it'll do you good. Yes, actually, I was half afraid he wouldn't go. I wouldn't have known what to do next. I'm the original ten-stone weakling.'

Andrea's smile was warm and affectionate. 'You under-estimate yourself.'

'Not really. Well let's hope I don't have to prove myself again. He might discover I'm just a fraud.'

'I can't tell you how much I appreciate your coming here, David.'

'When I said I'd try to help you, I never expected to have to get involved in that way. Just point you in the right direction to get the legal situation sorted out. The sooner the better, I feel, now I've seen him. An injunction keeping him away from you, and a divorce - as soon as possible.'

'And then?' murmured Andrea.

'I've been on to my divorce lawyer friend, Charlotte Saville-Banks, and if you want to see her in the office, she'll get her secretary to fit you in.'

'That's kind,' said Andrea twisting the glass in her hand.

'But, in view of what's happened, I think we should go and have a chat with her tonight. I'm sure she won't mind. As I told you, the other day, she's an old friend from university.'

She knew he was aware of her tension and that much of what he was saying was to relax her.

'No glamour girl - I never saw her out of jeans. She was a bit large too. But we all used to have a lot of fun together, as you do at college. I haven't seen her much recently. She married one of the rugby team who drank rather a lot, and had an unpleasant marriage break up herself. That was when I was going through my own particular hell.' He paused for a moment, as if his mind had taken him to another place. 'But she was pleased to hear from me when I rang. When I told her all about you, she said she thought I wasn't interested in women now.'

'And aren't you?' asked Andrea, blushing and looking down at the glass.

'Don't play games with me, Andrea. You know I'm in love with you. I think I fell in love with you the first time I saw you.'

Andrea smiled at his words. Sometimes you couldn't believe that your hopes would come true. She said nothing for a moment, thinking back to the day when she first met David, and remembering all that had gone before. How glad she had been to have a place that she could regard as a refuge. She never imagined what it would lead to. When she saw the advert in the paper shop, she knew it would give her a little bit of independence and for that she was thankful. And when she arrived at the house, she was sure she could make it homely. She could tell it had been cared for before - that a woman had looked after it.

On the mantelpiece was a wedding photo, a young couple, he thin and gangling, the woman rosy, her face full of smiles. The young man, Andrea had decided, was the son of the house. His father - in her imagination, a tall, distinguished man with silver hair - was the person who had advertised for a cleaning lady. 'Widower requires domestic help' - it had conjured up a picture of a sixty or seventy year old.

Even so, the young man in the photo seemed to smile at her as she dusted.

David applied a dressing to the wound with a deft hand. 'I'll never forget seeing you for the first time. I remember coming home because I'd forgotten my Filofax. I walked in, and saw this woman sitting on the floor crying. You looked up and I saw a bruise on your face. I put two and two together, and thought - how could anyone hurt that beautiful woman? There was the scent of lavender in the air. That's when I realised who you were.'

For the moment, Andrea didn't know what to say.

'Oh, David,' she breathed.

For so long their relationship had been formal - as formal as it could be - for his sympathetic manner kept slipping into the most mundane conversations and she found it hard to contain her feelings of attraction to him. Now what he said couldn't be ignored. She, too, remembered that day when she first saw him - when the young man in the wedding photograph came alive for her.

David carried on talking, and it was as if, now he had started, it all had to come out.

'And, after that, I noticed the smell of lavender every time you'd been. And then I had a picture of you in my mind. And I couldn't get it out of my head.'

Andrea felt dizzy for the moment. Could this all be true? Did he just want a fling with an older woman? She had to be sure about his feelings.

'It's lovely that you should say that,' she said. 'But there's nearly eight years' difference between us. You heard what Justin said - "Toy boy". I'm afraid I'm too old for you. People will say I'm an old hag, cradle snatching.'

David stroked her fair hair with a gentle hand. 'You're so lovely, Annie. How could anyone think that? They'd think I was lucky to have you. Anyway, what does it matter what the rest of the world thinks? When two people are right for each other, age doesn't come into it.'

She was aware of her voice shaking. 'I want it to be true. But I have to be sure. You've been a wonderful friend and I don't want to lose that friendship. I don't want any more mistakes in my life. You loved Sarah, and now you say you love me. What about the other women since Sarah? There must have been others.'

'I warded them off after Sarah died. Not that many of them regarded me as the model for a centrefold, I'm sure.'

She smiled, because he was quite unaware of how attractive he was.

'They all seemed to want to mother me. All I wanted was to be left alone. I didn't want a mother. I didn't want another wife. I just wanted Sarah back. I missed her so much. She was my lover and my best friend. I didn't want a relationship with anyone else.'

'That's why I don't want you to rush into something you'll regret.'

'I've moved on, Annie, I don't feel the same pain any more. It's true I didn't want anyone at first. There were several women who offered to come and do things around the house, friends of Sarah, friends from Uni - their sympathy was unbearable. Strangers were easier. That's why I advertised for cleaning help. You were ideal. Totally anonymous. A happily married woman, I thought.'

'You found out the truth about that!'

'But by that time it didn't matter any more. In any case, Annie, it meant a lot to me coming home and finding everything looking nice. Sarah used to be house-proud like you. After she'd gone, I tried to keep it the way she would have wanted. I'd go round the house every Saturday.'

He got up and walked round the room, almost as if he were enacting his former routine. Andrea watched him, wondering if the love she felt for him would be sufficient to assuage the pain of the past.

'I'd hoover and dust and clean the kitchen floor,' he continued. 'I'd throw all the sheets and towels in the washing machine and get them dry on Sunday. It was disciplined, but there were no frills. After she died, I missed her touches. I missed the warmth and the smell and the homeliness. All the things that were part of her before, and all the things that reminded me how much I missed her.'

He sat down again, his expression, for the moment, far away.

'It was good of you to take me on trust,' Andrea said, and his eyes returned to her.

'I have a confession. I asked at the paper shop if they knew you.'

'Really? What did they say?'

'That you were a lovely lady. So I wasn't much the wiser. But that seemed enough for me to know. Though when you first posted that note to me, asking for the job, I tried to analyse your handwriting. '

'I didn't want to talk on the phone in case it was anyone I knew.'

'I used to look at all your little memos and guess at what you were like from the slant and the loops. At first I decided you were a frustrated career woman with a young child.'

'Fancy trying to analyse my boring notes.'

'But there was no evidence of a child. And the notes were a bit down to earth, so I changed my mind about that.'

Andrea remembered how, in her eagerness to remain anonymous, she had succeeded in erasing any trace of personality from her notes, saying things like, 'Clean sheets in the linen cupboard. Have polished the candlesticks.' It was still surprising to her that David could have had any interest in the uninspiring person who wielded the vacuum cleaner and wrote such comments.

'Then I started to have this charlady image in my mind - a bit like someone from Coronation Street, with a pinny and a scarf round your hair.'

'No-one looks like that nowadays, David.'

'Then when you put that slice of meat pie in the fridge, I got a new image.'

The almost empty fridge had been a pitiful sight for Andrea. Perhaps because of the despair in her own life, she had viewed the contents of the fridge, belonging, as she thought, to an elderly bereaved man, as particularly touching. The tiny bag of frozen peas, a frozen pizza one day, a frozen pie the next. She had decided to bring a home cooked meal into the life of this lonely man.

'That pie was the best thing I'd tasted for a year. As I heated it up, the house smelled as if Sarah was at home there again. I so rarely use the oven - nearly always the microwave. After I'd eaten, I tried to pretend she was in the kitchen washing up. But all I could think was that she'd betrayed me, she'd walked out on me.'

'But she died,' protested Andrea.

'Yes, but I felt so angry with her for leaving me behind. She had no right to go. She was only twenty three. We thought we had all those years together - children - holidays - problems - schools - even growing old. We thought we were going to share so many things. Why did she take such a chance, pulling out when the road wasn't clear?'

'She wouldn't have wanted to leave you, David,' said Andrea, tears in her eyes.

'After that meal, I sat down and cried. It was the first time for ages. I hadn't cried since the funeral. And I picked up that empty plate and threw it across the room.'

Andrea couldn't speak. She could tell how deep his despair had been. How could he love her, when he had loved Sarah so much?

'Then I went to bed and tried to remember what it was like when we were making love. And all I could feel was an ache, a constant ache. Like a limb had been torn from me.'

'Oh David, if only I'd known it would just cause you more pain.'

'But it was wonderful, Andrea. I could feel all your warmth and kindness in that meal. I had to change my idea of you once again. Got it wrong again, of course. I decided you were chubby and motherly. The pinny turned into a crisp apron, and you were bustling and brisk. But the meal was wonderful. I had to thank you.'

'I remember. Your note said, "Your pastry nearly floated me to heaven." What a romantic way to write.'

'And you wrote back an embarrassed stiff little note, saying, "Would you mind if I buy some lavender polish?"'

'I didn't mean to sound cold. Things had got so bad at home. But your house was my little haven.'

'Was that why you bought the bunches of daffodils, sometimes?'

'Did you still think I was brisk and bustling?'

'I'd heard your voice on the telephone, by then. It surprised me. Your voice sounded so much younger than I'd imagined. Why did you ring me?'

'You'd left the house in such a mess.'

'D'you know what I thought then, Andrea? I thought you were going to give me your notice.'

'I was worried about you. It was so out of character. The unwashed crockery. The empty bottle. Glass all over the floor. The broken photo frame. The house looked like a bomb had hit it.'

'Yes, I remember. It was our anniversary - would have been our anniversary, I mean. Four years. I tried to drink myself silly. I threw our wedding photo across the room.'

'David. I know you love Sarah. You love her even now.'

'I'll never forget her. But all the bitterness I felt has evaporated. I feel privileged to love two special women.' David gently stroked her cheek. 'To me you're still a dream vision,' he said. 'I can't believe I'm lucky enough to have a second chance. You are going to give me that chance, Andrea, aren't you?'

She looked up at him, her face still somewhat melancholy and frightened. He put his arms round her and embraced her with gentleness, still hesitating, as if it might be a mistake. They looked again at each other, now a little surer of each other.

'Your glasses are steaming up,' said Andrea, her voice shaky.

'You're enough to get anyone steamed up,' David whispered.

Andrea smiled, put down her brandy and took off his glasses.

'Justin used to say I was an iceberg - he called me the original ice maiden,' she confessed.

'Then perhaps he just didn't know how to achieve a melt-down.'

'Always the physicist,' she laughed.

The arm of the chair was a barrier between them. In a single action, they both rose and moved towards each other and this time the kiss lasted longer. In a moment, they sank back on the chintz-covered settee.

It was forty minutes before the chiming of the grandmother clock disturbed them with eight strokes. They smiled at each other without embarrassment, no longer with the hesitance of lovers still unsure of each other.

'That cool lavender perfume you wear is a con-trick,' said David, wiping perspiration from his forehead with the back of his hand. 'Justin obviously didn't know that the major part of an iceberg is concealed. He didn't know your undiscovered depths. Just the same, I'd say Mount Vesuvius was a better description. Is there somewhere I can shower?'

'Yes, Professor. I'll take you upstairs,' replied Andrea, laughing at the description, but not moving from the settee. Picking up her no longer crisp white shirt with one hand, she linked her other hand with his.

'Andrea, I'd forgotten about taking you to Charlotte!' David exclaimed. 'Now we know where we're going, let's get things started. I know she'll want to arrange a meeting in the office, but I'd like you to meet her informally this evening. She's very sympathetic with wife battering.'

They got up unsteadily. Andrea's feet encountered a bottle, still on the floor where it had fallen.

'Oh, that wine,' said Andrea shrinking back. 'Whatever possessed him to bring it? I don't want any reminders of him around.'

'We'll take it to Charlotte, later,' said David, picking it up and placing it on the coffee table. 'A bottle of plonk in payment for unofficial advice is right up her street.'

Taking her hand, he allowed her to lead him from the room.

Chapter 8: Charlie Girl

(Thursday Night)

For a moment, when Charlotte heard footsteps on the pavement above her basement flat, she thought it was Stephanie. She finished chopping onions, scooped them into a frying pan and lit the gas. It was over an hour since Stephanie had telephoned. 'I'll be home late, Charlie. Don't worry about me,' she'd said, her soft little voice faint and indistinct.

Charlotte had gritted her teeth. Not worry. How could she help worrying when she thought of the state that Stephanie had been in, recently, whenever she came home late?

How many more times was she going to be embarrassed like last week, when she had phoned Stephanie's office after one of these episodes and told them that Stephie had an upset stomach?

'Not again,' the supercilious voice at the other end of the telephone had said.

She's not going to hold onto this job much longer, Charlotte had thought.

She had said as much to Stephanie once or twice already.

'Oh, there are always temp jobs for secretaries and WP operators,' Stephanie had replied airily.

Footsteps clattered down the stone steps that led to the flat. Charlotte jumped up, a smile of relief forming on her strong aristocratic face. But no, the sound obviously came from more than one person. Then came the tinkling note of the old-fashioned bell, a remnant of the Victorian era in which the house had been built.

She turned down the gas under the pan, which now smelled strongly of a mixture of garlic, tomatoes and onions, and went to open the front door. Instead of Stephanie, two people stood in the doorway.

'David, how nice to see you.'

Damn, she thought. I'd forgotten he said he'd pop in some time.

She was irritated that he'd come without warning, so that she had no opportunity to prepare herself. She was wearing a huge hand-knitted sweater and faded jeans, which she knew showed off her too large behind. She was sure that David had never seen her dressed any other way. She wished he had brought his woman friend to the office, where they would have found her looking quite smart, in a dark suit which made her appear slimmer, and with her hair up in a tidy pleat. To make matters worse, the woman beside David looked cool and composed, despite a dressing on the side of her face. Just the sort of person who made Charlotte feel edgy. Her fair hair was smoothed back and she wore an immaculate white tailored blouse and slim dark skirt.

Charlotte was tempted to give David a hug, as she had the last time they met, some months before but, without knowing the relationship between him and the woman, she felt inhibited.

'Can we come in, Charlie? Or are you busy?'

'Of course you can. Come in. Come in. Is this the friend you told me about on the telephone the other day?'

David made the introductions and Charlotte managed to sound interested and welcoming, even though she was already worrying that they would still be here when Stephanie arrived home.

'I'm expecting a friend in a little while. Do you mind if I carry on cooking? I was just making a pizza. Would you like something?'

Charlotte led them in through the narrow hall into the spacious kitchen, where the pizza dough was resting on a wooden table, liberally sprinkled with flour, and surrounded by what was left of the other ingredients.

She turned off the gas and then resumed kneading the dough with large, red capable hands, flexing her fingers, enjoying the responsive plasticity of the dough.

David placed a bottle of wine on an empty corner of the table. Charlotte felt her smile fade.

'Thanks, David. There's really no need. Do take it back.'

'Don't be stupid, Charlie. We come bursting in here, uninvited, when you're expecting someone. It's the least we can do.'

'Oh, very well,' she said, still not smiling. Wiping the flour off her hands, she took the bottle, opened a cupboard containing baking dishes and put it right at the back. She wondered if Stephanie would spot it there.

She tried to ignore the couple's puzzled look.

'You haven't given it up, have you, Charlie? You used to like coming out with the boys for a drink.'

'Having a jar with the boys. Yes, those were the days, David. No I haven't given up the demon drink.'

David refrained from mentioning it again. Charlotte felt relieved. She rolled out the dough and placed it on a tray.

'Now, some coffee. Stephanie won't be here for ages, so there's plenty of time for the pizza. She's my flatmate actually. But I usually cook, because she often works late.'

She put the kettle on, sneaking a glance at her watch as she did so, and put coffee into three mugs, each of them a statement of her philosophy. She selected *Join hands with the Greenham Common women* for Andrea and *Say No to Cruise Missiles* for David; her own mug, a tribute to a much earlier battle said, 'Votes for Women.' She poured the tomato mixture on to the pizza base, while she waited for the kettle to boil.

As the three of them sat at the kitchen table, David sketched in Andrea's problems and Charlotte listened with sympathy. She was outraged at Justin's behaviour and determined to give Andrea all the help she could. Andrea was less poised than she looked and Charlotte soon felt her own confidence returning.

'He must be a bastard. I know just how you feel. I had one like that. Leaving him was the best thing I ever did. Don't worry about the legal side. We'll talk about it in the office and I'll take you through every step of the way.'

'Do you deal with a lot of broken marriages?' Andrea asked.

'My dear! I've seen them all. There's nothing you can't tell me about marriage. I'm unshockable. I've seen behaviour you wouldn't believe from people who put up the most wonderful facade right until the end. I've seen wives who are nothing but prostitutes, doling out sex in return for kitchen gadgets and fancy clothes, and husbands, poor saps, innocently forking out for it all.'

'That's very cynical,' said Andrea, looking rather shocked.

'And then of course, there's the other side - well you and I both know about that - where a man thinks because he's married to you, he owns you, and that entitles him to treat you exactly how he likes. Thank goodness, the law is moving towards change in that aspect of marriage.'

'I suppose you got divorced yourself,' Andrea said.

'You bet your sweet life I did,' Charlotte replied with emphasis. 'I can tell you I've given the bastards a wide berth since then. I should have known better than to get married in the first place. My father and my husband were two of a kind. Dad beat my mother up and me, too. There's very few like our David here. Now he *is* a New Man. Sarah was a lucky girl to get him.'

'Not so lucky,' David reminded her.

'No, poor child,' said Charlotte, remembering the young college friend who had so prematurely met her death. 'All her life ahead of her.' To her embarrassment, she felt tears come to her eyes. Involuntarily she burst out, 'I hope you find happiness again, David. You deserve it.'

'I already have,' he replied, brushing Andrea's hand with the tips of his fingers.

Charlotte caught the movement, smiled a little at them both and, feeling suddenly superfluous, glanced at her watch again in a more noticeable gesture.

David, obviously aware of her anxiety, said, 'We must let you get on with your cooking.'

Charlotte picked up the pizza and placed it in the oven. 'Sorry I'm rather tense,' she excused herself to David. 'It's just that I'm a bit worried about Stephanie. She's not normally so late.' She realised she had contradicted herself and rushed to change the subject. 'You and I must get together again – and your friend too. Socially, I mean. We'll have lunch, when you've arranged an appointment at my office. Mention it to my secretary.'

Filled with relief, now that they were going, Charlotte walked to the door with them and, with her warmth for David once again welling up, she caught his hand and gave it an affectionate squeeze.

She watched them as they climbed up the stairs to pavement level, and, in a gently ironic tone, called after them, 'Bless you, my children.'

Through the railings, she saw a taxi draw up in front of the house. She saw David walk a few yards ahead of Andrea to the car, getting his keys out. Thank goodness he didn't see Stephanie, as she got out of the taxi, a coat draped round her thin figure, swaying slightly as she walked towards the basement steps. Charlotte saw her staring at Andrea with undisguised animosity and Andrea, embarrassed, turned away and followed David to the car.

The blonde girl descended the steps, calling in a too loud voice, 'Charlie. I'm here. Let me in. I can't find my key.'

Charlotte pulled her through the open door, her fingers digging into Stephanie's thin upper arms.

'Stop it. You're hurting me,' said Stephanie, shaking herself free and walking with unsteady steps towards the kitchen. She allowed her coat to slip off her shoulders on to the floor, revealing her patterned blouse in disarray, buttons incorrectly done up and her skirt swivelled round and unzipped.

'Where have you been?' The fear and apprehension in Charlotte's voice made the question come out in a high pitched, almost hysterical screech.

'I've been having a nice time, which you won't let me have,' replied Stephanie, slurring the words.

'You're drunk.'

'I had drinks with one of the reps. He gave me three G & Ts and then I got laid. And then I had some more, for being a good girl.'

Charlotte went white.

'You don't mean that. You're just saying it.'

'I told him I'd do anything for a drink, and he said, "Anything?" I said "Anything." So he took me into the exec., exec.' she stumbled over the words. 'Executive suite and found some drinks. And then we did it on the desk. Big, big desk. He could do all sorts of things that you can't do.'

Charlotte slapped her hard across the face.

Swaying drunkenly, Stephanie started to cry.

'I think I'm going to be sick.'

She rushed into the kitchen and vomited into the sink, panting and retching at each new wave of nausea.

Charlotte followed her, tears running down her cheeks. She found a damp cloth and wiped the other woman's face and, putting her arm round her, fed her like a child with sips of water from a spoon.

Stephanie staggered to a chair and sat down shakily at the kitchen table.

'I'll make you some coffee, Stephie. You'll feel better soon.'

The aromatic smell of pizza broke in on her thoughts. It was ready. Charlotte took it from the oven, and placed it on a dish on the table. Taking out clean mugs, she poured some more hot coffee for them both.

Stephanie sipped and began to recover.

'Oh, Charlie. I'm sorry. I'm so, so sorry. I hated it really. I did it for the booze. You wouldn't let me have any. I get desperate. Couldn't I have just a little one now? It would make me feel better. Just a little glass of wine, or brandy. To perk me up.

Charlotte hardened her heart.

'We haven't any in the house,' she lied. 'Why did you say that he was good?'

'I just said it to make you jealous. I saw that smart woman who came out of here. Who was she?'

'You fool. She wasn't anything to me. Just a client. Here with her boyfriend. He's an old friend. No-one matters to me except you. Don't you know that?'

'You're so good to me, Charlie.'

Charlotte got a basin and filled it with warm water. Taking the flannel, once again, she started sponging Stephanie's face and neck, smoothing the ash blonde hair out of the way. The shirt was stained with vomit and she carefully unbuttoned it and discarded it on the floor.

Stephanie held out her arms, her eyes entreating, and Charlotte abandoned the sponge and caught hold of her lover in her arms, her large bosom enveloping the other woman's slim figure.

Their faces were both wet with tears, as they kissed.

'Oh Charlotte, you're so good for me. How could any man match up to you?'

The pizza grew cold on the table.

Chapter 9: Tombola

(Friday Morning)

George Harkness was about to drive his car into a short term parking space, when a woman in a well-used Mini beat him to it. He growled under his breath, 'Women! They're everywhere. And always where you don't want them to be.'

There was his wife, Joan, saying 'Go and get me a loaf from the bakery in the High Street,' just as he was settling down with the Telegraph. 'You'll have to go early if you don't want to queue,' she had said, but he suspected it was just a ploy to get him out of the house, so that she could listen to Desert Island Discs without him interrupting with the news items of the day. She hadn't even remembered it was his birthday. Come to that, neither had Elaine. You would have thought she'd have sent a card to her father, even though she was such a busy career woman these days. Still, creeping old age wasn't necessarily something to celebrate. In fact, what could be worse? A birthday and retirement in the space of a fortnight.

With care, he reversed the car away from the occupied space, his eyes on the mirror. Now he would probably have to do a complete circuit of the one way system, or go to the multi-storey. At the rev of another car engine, he glanced forward again. A young chap pulling out next to the Mini gave him a thumb's up. After all, his luck was in.

Shooting into the space fast, before anyone else could take it, he found himself perilously close to the Mini, which was over the line. In fact, he couldn't open the driver's side door without hitting it. He would have an embarrassing struggle over the gear levers in order to get out on the other side, unless he took a chance and waited for the woman to go.

He glanced at the Mini again. The woman was leaning across to lock the car from the inside. Damn, the face was familiar - it was that solicitor woman with a double barrelled name who worked in the office next to his. Charlotte something or other. Large, overpowering creature - and her practice always filled with hysterical women. He winced at the memory.

He was forced to carry out a wriggling manoeuvre across the various protrusions, because the damn woman was waiting - probably to make sure he didn't mark her door.

Charlotte had got out of her car and was straightening her black office skirt. Her face looked rather pale against her dark hair, bunched at the back in a severe office style. George debated whether or not to ignore her.

She took the decision out of his hands.

'Good morning, Mr Harkness,' she called, as he locked the car with the electronic remote switch. 'I haven't seen you at the office, recently.'

'I retired last week,' he growled.

'I wouldn't have thought you were old enough,' she said, sounding surprised. 'What a terrible waste of all your knowledge and experience.'

He was genuinely flattered. She wasn't the type to make that sort of comment unless she meant it. He warmed towards her a little and they strode off in the same direction.

'I don't know what I'm going to do with myself, Miss, er, Ms, er, Charlotte. I'm reduced to running errands for my wife. It's driving me mad already.'

'Well, I certainly hope you'll find some outlet for your talent, Mr Harkness. I don't believe in ageism, any more than I do in sexism. Our advice centre could always do with some voluntary help.'

'Thank you. I'll bear that in mind,' George said, mentally comparing the pack of women at the advice centre with the potent one at home. Looking for some means of changing the subject, he noticed a bottle shaped object under her arm. 'You having a celebration this morning?'

'I was going to find a home for it.' Her voice now sounded embarrassed. 'We - I'm allergic to red wine.'

'Well, don't throw it away.' He waggled a finger at the building they were approaching. 'There's the very place.'

George often passed the church, so near to his old office, and liked its ageing appearance, contrasting with the modern buildings surrounding it. Today it was teeming with activity.

'CHURCH RESTORATION FUND, BRING & BUY - 10 O'CLOCK,' said a large notice. Helpers were setting up stalls in the hall inside.

Next to the church, they saw a shape in a doorway of an empty shop. A man in a filthy overcoat was sleeping there. His hair was wild and his face dirty and unshaven. An empty bottle lay near him in the alcove.

'Disgusting,' George exclaimed. 'These down-and-outs - they're just human litter.'

Charlotte shuddered at the man's appearance.

'Who knows what takes people along that route?' she said and there was a tremor in her voice. 'There, but for the grace of God, go you and I, Mr Harkness - or our loved ones, perhaps. Are you sure you think I should donate this bottle to the church? Isn't it the cause of that man's downfall?'

'I can't answer that, my dear girl. But people have to help themselves in this world. There are places available - your advice centre - you're giving people support. Alcoholics Anonymous - that's another kind of help. People have to get off their back-sides and go and look for help, if they can't do something on their own.'

'Alcoholics Anonymous,' said Charlotte frowning. 'I hadn't thought...' Her voice trailed off.

'But I really think this chap here is beyond help,' George continued.

'I suppose it would be irresponsible of me to put this bottle in the bin,' said Charlotte ruefully.

'Another nail in the coffin for someone like him,' George commented. 'Just a pleasant little social habit for most people.'

He glanced at Charlotte. Her face looked so serious that he was suddenly aware that the old man was not the only subject of her concern. He patted her on the shoulder. 'Given the right help and support, some alcoholics make a marvellous recovery.'

'I suppose removing temptation is a step in the right direction,' she said. 'I'd better take this into the church. There's bound to be a raffle or something. Nice talking to you, Mr Harkness. Don't forget to drop into the advice centre some time.'

She smiled surprisingly warmly at him and then, turning away, walked with upright swinging gait towards the grey stone building, the bottle in her hand.

George watched the retreating rear with a degree of admiration. He'd always had a weakness for bottoms, as one or two of his secretaries had found out. Not that he'd ever got involved in - what did these feminists call it? Sexual harassment? He didn't need to. You could soon tell when a woman was giving you the come-on. His last secretary had made a point of coming into his office and bending over his filing cabinet, her low cut blouse revealing such an abundance of inviting flesh it was difficult to decide which end of her to look at. It certainly added a small frisson to the office days, which he missed a great deal. A gentle pat on the behind had originally led to their out of office affair, which he was also missing now. She too had retired and gone with her husband to make a new life in the West Country, and the delicious naughtiness, which affected neither spouse, had been curtailed with reluctance on both sides.

George strolled along to the popular bakery, collected a loaf and returned to his car. He climbed in and drove down the street. Only five minutes away from the busy shopping centre was the quiet tree lined road in which he lived. He pulled up in front of an elegant detached house.

'I'm home, dear,' he said, opening the front door.

Joan was bending over the washing machine as George walked into the kitchen. He was about to give her an affectionate pat, when some apparent sixth sense caused her to straighten up.

'Did you get the bread?'

'Yes. I got a French loaf.'

'You know white bread isn't good for you. You need the fibre.'

'I thought it would make a nice change,' George defended himself.

'I hope you're not going to interfere with the way I run things, now you're home all the time.'

He sighed.

'Goodness knows, Joan, the last thing I want is to encroach on your domain.'

'As long as you know I'm not intending to change my routine. I managed when you were at the office, and I'll carry on managing. Why don't you take up golf or something, now that you're at a loose end?'

'I thought we'd do things together,' he said, a little hurt at her eagerness to find him outside occupations. And she still hadn't remembered the birthday.

'Well, of course we'll be doing some things together,' she relented. 'But not all the time.'

George sat himself down and picked up the paper.

'Before you settle down...,' she said.

He looked up.

'I've got a confession to make.'

'Yes?'

'I meant to send some bits and bobs for the church sale, and I completely forgot.'

'You don't really expect me to go back again. Your bits and pieces can't be that important. Give them to a charity shop.'

'George, I *promised* the vicar. I can't let him down. And – there is another reason.'

'Well, what is it?'

'Betty's popping over for coffee. We've got some new recipes to discuss. You won't want to be bothered with us girls and our gossip, will you? But I'll make a really nice lunch, so get home at twelve thirty.'

She dumped two carrier bags of clothes at George's feet and he put down the paper and glowered. He didn't argue - just picked them up and left the house. He couldn't believe her charitable donations were that important. He wondered, for a moment if she had a lover, rather than a visiting neighbour, but that at least made him laugh. The truth was, she just wanted to get rid of him. He'd been evicted.

Feeling angry and impotent, he went back to the high street. He found a parking place. He stomped into the church, and delivered the carrier bags to a pair of willing arms, aware of being amongst a large quantity of young mothers and middle aged women. He noted the paucity of men of any age. Where did they all go? What did they do when their working lives were over and their wives didn't want or need them?

The vicar approached him. No doubt he appreciated seeing another male.

'Ah, Mr Harkness. I'm so glad that you're supporting us. Have you bought a ticket for the tombola?'

George took out some change and dipped into the container of tickets. One of them was a winning number and rewarded him with a jar of pickle.

'Thought I might get the champagne, Vicar. Though goodness knows I haven't got much to celebrate.'

The vicar's face became solicitous. 'Not problems with the family, I hope, Mr Harkness. I was so sorry to hear of your daughter's divorce.'

'Well that's water under the bridge now, Vicar. She's making a new life for herself. No, I'm afraid I'm being entirely selfish. I'm an active man and I don't know what to do with myself. I've only been retired a week and it's driving me round the bend!'

'DIY?' suggested the vicar, his voice hesitant.

'You must be joking.'

'Bridge, perhaps.'

'Vicar, I don't need pastimes. I want a whole new life. I want something to get my teeth into.'

The vicar looked at him over the top of his half-glasses. 'It was rather remiss of your company to let you go without any retirement preparation, Mr Harkness.'

'They had seminars,' growled George. 'To tell you the truth, Vicar, I couldn't take any interest. I didn't feel as if it was really going to happen.'

'Retirement doesn't suit everyone, Mr Harkness. But let's keep things in perspective. It's a problem, not a tragedy.'

'And how am I going to solve it, Vicar?'

The vicar scratched his head. 'Mr Harkness, I will look around, though I have to say that nothing springs immediately to mind. There are so many people with more acute problems at the moment. Recession, house repossessions. One sees terrible tragedies caused by debt.' He lowered his voice slightly. 'Take that young man over there.' He nodded in the direction of a thin worried youth, pouring over second hand children's clothes. 'His wife's just had a baby.

He's lost his job. No money coming in. How can we help someone like that?'

'Those sort of problems need careful management. Isn't there some sort of financial advice centre where you can send him?'

'I've recommended the Citizens Advice Bureau, though I know they're overwhelmed with people with the same problem. They need more expert help themselves.'

He stopped short and stared at George.

'That's an inspiration, Vicar. That's somewhere I might be needed.'

He strolled around the hall thinking, and browsing through the products on sale at the same time. There were some home baked cakes, but he dared not take any of those, or Joan might think he was getting at her. The white elephant stall revealed some old china that was rather attractive, and he wondered if he should start collecting antiques and visit the Antiques Roadshow. But most of the stuff on display was decidedly tatty. He hurried past the pile of musty smelling second hand clothes.

It was no use. He couldn't kill any more time here. George ambled towards the door, past the tombola stall which was almost the only thing worth putting money into. He felt embarrassed to be leaving so quickly. 'I'll have some more tickets,' he said holding out a pound to the Vicar.

'Two hundred and nine. That's a winner. The bottle of red wine someone brought in this morning. That's poetic justice; she said you told her to donate it,' said the Vicar, obviously pleased with this outcome.

George peered at the label on the bottle. Reading glasses or their absence were another irritation brought on by the passing years. He could just make out a heart and arrow motif, but it wasn't a logo he recognised.

He wandered out and, placing the wine in his car, strolled on to the library. He was not a great reader, but the thought of returning so soon to Joan and her friend was off-putting.

He walked up to the librarian, a blonde woman of about thirty with an ample bosom, kept in check by a severely buttoned blouse.

'Have you got the book of that TV serial that was on some time back - can't remember the name - about this middle-aged man - bit of a rough diamond - that has an affair with a University lecturer.'

'"Nice Work",' replied the librarian without hesitation.

'Nice work if you can get it,' said George, giving her a meaningful wink.

'The book is called "Nice Work",' said the librarian. She returned his twinkle with a cold glance.

'Snooty bitch,' murmured George. 'The woman in the story, I mean. Where will I find it?'

The book in hand, he returned it to her for stamping. 'Oh, by the way, where's the CAB office? Is it round here?'

'Right next door,' answered the woman. 'But I doubt if they can help you with your problem.'

He laughed and made a mental note to return. He liked a woman with a bit of spirit. And the buttons on that blouse were almost asking to be undone.

He looked at his watch. Lunch at twelve thirty. There was still plenty of time to call in at the Citizens' Advice Bureau.

It was literally the building next door. A pleasant middle aged woman was just about to put up a closed sign.

'We're closed until two thirty now, sir.'

'But it's not even midday yet.'

'Yes sir, we can't get the advisers.'

'Well, that's the very reason I'm here. Your luck is in. I've come to help.'

'Hold on a minute. What sort of help are you offering?' she asked, smiling, an engaging dimple appearing in her cheek.

'Well, I'm - I was an accountant. Financial help or advice, I suppose.'

'Financial advice.' Her eyes gleamed. 'Look no further. We could certainly do with that sort of help. Since interest rates rocketed, we're getting a mass of people coming in with terrible debts. Most of them have no idea how to sort themselves out.'

He relaxed and smiled.

'When can I come?' he asked.

'It's not that simple. I'll have to arrange for a panel interview.'

'I was hoping we could talk about it now.' George said, used to getting his own way.

'Look, I've got a lot of paperwork to get through - that's why I was shutting up shop - but I could give you a broad idea of some of the problems we're dealing with. If you've got a half an hour now, we could have a cup of coffee and talk about it.'

His smile broadened. He felt instinctively they were going to have a good working relationship.

He arrived back home in much better spirits. He was surprised to see his daughter's car in the drive.

'Joan, I'm home. Is that Elaine's car outside?'

'You're late,' replied his wife, coming into the hall. 'We were worried about you. Elaine and Alex have come to join us for a birthday lunch.'

His daughter followed her mother out of the dining room and hugged him, and her small son approached, fists at the ready for a ritual exchange of punches.

'My birthday. I'd forgotten,' he lied, ruffling the boy's hair, pleased that he had been wrong. 'We can celebrate with this bottle of wine that I won.'

'I can do better than that,' said his wife. 'I've got some champagne.'

He followed the women into the dining room. The table was laid for lunch with the bone china dinner set and silver cutlery, which they saved for special occasions. A platter of dressed salmon, a dish of asparagus tips and bowls of various other salads met his eyes. The champagne rested in a bucket of ice.

'Well, you've pushed the boat out,' he exclaimed, now really surprised.

'I didn't mean to be unkind this morning,' said Joan smiling. 'I just wanted a chance to get everything ready. And of course, it is more difficult to do things with someone under your feet.'

She was a good wife, really, George thought; she was like the salmon - good quality plain fare. One could say she just lacked a little mayonnaise but, fortunately, his additional activities acted as the dressing and enhanced their marriage.

He smiled at his wife, warmly, guiltlessly.

'Why don't you open the champagne, George? Did you get any ideas while you were out?'

The cork shot across the room and George poured the sparkling liquid into the waiting glasses.

'Yes, I've been digging around a bit and I've got a few new ideas. Might even involve some evening work,' he added, wondering how long the librarian would take to loosen up.

'Well, that's wonderful. Happy birthday, George,' said Joan, lifting her glass.

Elaine raised her glass and said, turning to her parents, 'To your future and new interests.'

George smiled, a small twinkle in his eye. 'Bottoms up.'

The trio clinked glasses.

Chapter 10: Going Solo

(Friday)

'I'm glad you brought Alex over,' Joan said. 'Your father loves having his grandson here. Makes him feel young again, playing those boys' games.'

They were in the kitchen loading the dishwasher, whilst George and Alex were indulging in a noisy game of cricket in the garden.

'Does that mean he was disappointed that he only had a daughter?'

'Now you know better than that, Elaine. You always were the apple of his eye.'

She means he spoiled me, thought Elaine, without commenting. Her instincts told her that her mother was leading the conversation towards some sort of a lecture and she should find some way of diverting her.

She closed the dishwasher and smiled, 'Shall we treat ourselves to a cup of tea, whilst the boys are having fun?'

'Good idea,' replied Joan, filling the kettle and placing some cups ready. 'Of course, he misses Tony. He was really upset at your divorce.'

So the conversation was headed in the usual direction. It was one of her mother's, "You never had it so good, so why did you let him go?" lectures.

'I wouldn't have been able to bring Alex, if it hadn't been half term holiday,' she commented, again trying diversionary tactics.

'I wondered why he wasn't at school. How did you manage during the week? You know you could have brought him here.'

'I took two or three days off work, and of course he's been with friends as well. He likes to be in his own home. He has enough disruption.' The words were out before she could stop them. Cue for mother.

'Divorce is always hard on children, especially at his age. Young people today don't work hard enough at it. Didn't Tony have him this holiday?' Joan asked.

'Tony's collecting him tonight and having him for the weekend.' Elaine sat down at the kitchen table.

'He's a good father.'

'I've never disputed that.'

'You should have hung on to him. Women have to turn a blind eye to a small indiscretion.'

'I suppose you mean a few small indiscretions.'

The kettle boiled and Joan poured the water into the teapot and brought it to the table. She put some assorted biscuits on a plate and sat down.

'You're so naive, Elaine. Men are different to women. Even the best of them have only one thing on their mind. Surely it's better to have a quiet life and let them get their needs sorted out somewhere else?'

Elaine picked up a bourbon biscuit and took an aggressive bite.

'I never had a problem with sex, Mother. I just didn't like Tony bringing someone else's perfume into my bedroom.'

'You didn't know when you were well off. You had a nice house. Plenty of money.' Joan poured some milk and tea into the cups. 'He never minded your spending it. He was generous to you and Alex. You always looked good. Now look at you.'

'Thank you,' said Elaine, tightening her lips.

'And you work all the hours God made. What sort of a life do you have?'

'I happen to like my job very much, Mother. And my independence.'

'Are you still taking sugar?'

'Yes please.'

'You should use saccharin. You'll put on weight.'

Elaine ignored this statement and took a Jaffa cake, before Joan continued.

'He had a lot of good ways, your Tony. Look, he sent your father a birthday card.'

'He is *not* my Tony, any more. Yes, I know he has a lot of superficial charm. That was always his speciality. Don't think I'm totally immune to it.' She paused to drink a mouthful of tea. 'But I am not going back to the life I had with him. Disappearing for hours on end, and telling me lies about where he was. Why, he even brought one of his women home once, when he thought I was going to be out all day.'

'How do you know that?'

'When I came in, Tony came to the door all flustered. The kitchen door slammed and then I heard a car drive off. Later, I found her French knickers in our bed.'

Joan sniffed and changed tack.

'So you're off men for life.'

'I didn't say that.'

'Well, why don't you go out a bit more? You're not going to meet many men on a woman's magazine.'

'You'd be surprised how many men work there,' smiled Elaine. 'Anyway, I told you, I'm getting away for the weekend. I'm off to stay with Ginnie, tonight, once Tony's collected Alex.'

'Ginnie?'

'Yes, you remember, mother. Ginnie Lawson. Virginia.'

'Oh yes. I remember now. Quite a nice family, the Lawsons. Well, all I can say is if you're going off there for the weekend, you'd better smarten yourself up a bit. Didn't she have a brother? Why don't you wear some nice green eye shadow instead of that dull grey? It would bring out the colour of your eyes.'

'I just happen to prefer subtlety.' Elaine felt her patience wearing thin, now. 'And the brother works in France.'

'I'm only telling you for your own good,' Joan scolded. 'And as a matter of fact, you want to take more care of your skin. You redheads have very dry skin. You should use some Oil of Ulay. I've got some upstairs. I'll get it for you.'

'Mother, for heaven's sake, stop trying to organise me. I'm a grown woman now.'

'I'm only trying to help. If you're not careful, you'll get lines and by the time you're my age, you'll look ten years older. Your grandmother had that sort of gingerish hair, and her face was like old parchment. You just put a little on night and morning.'

Elaine stopped smiling and tried to restrain her temper.

'No Oil of Ulay, mother. READ MY LIPS.'

'Why do you use that silly expression?'

'It was good enough for George Bush. I thought you favoured the Republicans.'

'I'm afraid he hasn't got Ronald Reagan's charisma - a poor substitute - and *you* might find the same problem when you're looking for a new man to replace Tony.'

Elaine stood up. 'Whatever you say, Mother.' She'd have to get out before she started screaming. Somehow she managed to sound conversational. 'Anyway, I shall have to go soon. I've got a hundred and one things to do. I've got to get my case packed and sort out some things for Alex before Tony arrives this evening; and I want to pop into the off-licence for some wine for Ginnie, too.'

'Oh, you needn't bother to do that. You can take that bottle of wine your father won. It's very nice, I'm sure, but you know how red wine upsets my stomach. And we've still got the champagne. You take it. You'll be doing me a favour.'

Elaine was sapped of all resistance. Red wine was better than Oil of Ulay. It was one way of keeping her mother quiet.

'That's very kind of you, Mother. Just the same, I'd better call Alex in. I want to have him ready when Tony comes.'

I don't want to give him an excuse to hang around, she thought, but refrained from saying it out loud.

She took the wine from her mother and called to her father and son through the kitchen window, 'Dad, Alex, we've got to go shortly. Is the game nearly finished?'

It was still half an hour before she and Alex were ready to leave. She saw her mother watching her as she walked from the house, looking for signs of weariness to confirm her own disappointment at Elaine's changed situation. Elaine could almost imagine her mother's thoughts as she watched her daughter – *such a pity she'd sacrificed everything for her principles, instead of listening to good advice.*

She sent Alex to sort out his things as soon as they got home and she threw a few items of casual wear into a weekend case for herself.

The telephone call from Ginnie came just as Elaine had taken her leisure pants suit from the wardrobe. Alex, engrossed in packing some cars and miniature road menders into a box, ignored it, and Elaine, clad in her black lace slip, picked up the bedroom telephone.

'I know you've been looking forward to a quiet weekend and a natter,' came Ginnie's familiar voice. 'But, out of the blue, guess who's arriving tonight? My brother, Stephen. You remember him, don't you?'

'How could I forget him? He was the first man to break my heart,' commented Elaine dryly.

'Oh, surely not - I thought he was only interested in oily motor bikes then. Though not any more! Very suave, these days. Anyway, I thought we'd have a little dinner party. I telephoned my sister, Sally, and she'll probably be coming. So can you bring a dress for dinner tonight?' Elaine couldn't help a little sigh escaping. 'Don't worry, we'll still have time for our walk tomorrow - and a hack in the afternoon. I won't let them interfere in our girls' talk.'

'Damn!' said Elaine, putting down the phone. 'That's the last thing I wanted.'

'Are you talking about me?' came a familiar voice behind her.

Elaine jumped. The voice which she had always found seductive had not lost its appeal. The instinctive pleasure at the sound of it fought with irritation at hearing it now in her bedroom and lost the battle.

'What the hell are you doing in here, Tony?'

'Alex let me in. I came up to say hallo. I couldn't just walk out of the house taking him with me. You'd be claiming I'd abducted him. Don't I get a kiss?'

'Don't be ridiculous. You could have called out.'

'You were on the phone. You couldn't hear.'

'Well, you might at least have knocked on the door.'

His face expressed genuine puzzlement. 'Why? It's nothing I haven't seen before.'

'Look, Tony. You've given up your rights to all you see before you. And that includes rights to walk into my bedroom. If you would care to go downstairs and get Alex's stuff into the car, I will come down to see him off - when I have my clothes on.'

'I can't see why you're making such a fuss. I've seen far more flesh on the average Spanish package tour. You always did over-react.'

'Will you go downstairs? I want to change and you're making me late.'

'Shall I take your weekend case downstairs for you?' Tony asked, smiling at her with his usual charm.

'I haven't finished. I have to find a dress for a dinner party as well.'

'Oh, wear the little black dress. You always look very sexy in black. And black tights.'

'Thanks for the advice. You've obviously been learning from my mother.'

'Now there's a woman with an instinctive grasp of the average man's needs.'

Elaine couldn't help laughing at this. 'That's not how I've heard you describe your ex-mother-in-law before.'

'I know we've not always seen eye to eye, but she dropped one or two hints that she understands the difference between a casual affair and the real thing.'

'And which category do I come under?'

'You know you're the only woman for me. I'd be back like a shot if you'd have me.'

'With or without the casual affairs?'

'They're not important. Some people drink too much. Some can't help gambling. I can't stay away from women. It's just the excitement of forbidden fruit.' He discounted the episodes with a casual movement of his hands. 'Just think what it would mean to Alex - to have us back together.'

He was so persuasive and he knew her weakest point. She put aside temptation.

'I couldn't even consider it,' she lied. 'I know just how much it hurt me before.' That was the truth. 'I couldn't put up with that humiliation again. I have self-respect now.'

He reached out and touched her face.

'Self-respect. It doesn't keep you warm at night.'

He moved closer and took her in his arms. She felt the familiarity of his body. Temptation swept over her again. It was like the desire to lie down and sleep in the snow, even though it could kill you.

She let him kiss her.

'Don't go off for the weekend. Let your mother look after Alex. We could have a second honeymoon. Paris in the spring. I've got some holiday due.'

'What about my job?'

'What would that matter if we were together again?'

Common sense reached her brain, like a douche of ice cold water.

She stepped backwards, putting her hands on his shoulders to keep him from taking hold of her again. 'My job is very important to me, Tony. It's my life. I'm making a new life for myself. Without you. Please don't try to hold on to me.'

She dropped her hands, and he smiled ruefully.

'It was worth a try. I miss you.'

'Daddy. Are you ready?' Alex's voice came from mid-stairs. His feet clomped up the remainder of the steps.

'Can I come in, Mummy?'

She slipped a dressing gown on and opened the door. 'Daddy's just coming, Alex. Have a lovely weekend. I'll see you Sunday night.'

'Are you and Daddy friends now, Mummy?'

'Daddy and I are good friends, Alex.'

'Couldn't we all live together again?'

Elaine knelt down to his level, and stroked his hair. Softly she said, 'I'm sorry, Alex. But Daddy and I would just fight if we lived together again. This way is better.'

She hugged him, and reached out for a tissue to wipe a small tear away from the corner of his eye.

Avoiding Tony's gaze, she smiled and her voice sounded young and bright even to her own ears.

'Off you go, boys. Have a good weekend.'

She watched from the bedroom window, as Tony carried Alex's small case to the car and Alex followed with his precious box of toys. Stupidly, ridiculously, there were tears in her eyes.

She blew her nose hard with the tissue and opened the wardrobe door, then slipped off the dressing gown and looked at her reflection in the mirror. Her face looked back at her above the black lace. One of those faces that gave no clue to the vulnerability of its owner. She looked sophisticated and composed. That was the image she would take with her to the dinner party. Tony was right about one thing. The little black dress would be ideal.

Chapter 11: After Eight

(Friday Evening)

There was no doubt about it, Elaine could look stunning when she wanted to, although perhaps the scene with Tony had acted as a small charge of electricity. Whatever the reason, as she entered the room, having discreetly left the bottle of wine with Ginnie's husband, James, her cheeks were flushed, her auburn hair had the sheen of silky fabric and the little black dress was alluring.

Ginnie was welcoming. 'Elaine, you look fabulous. Being fancy free obviously suits you. I can't think why you haven't found a new man.'

'I wouldn't be fancy free, if I had,' commented Elaine wryly. 'Have I ever told you that I enjoy my job?'

'I'm not suggesting for a moment that you should give up your bachelor-girl existence, but a bit of male company and, well, you know..., does add a certain frisson.'

'I sublimate my energies into producing a damn good magazine. Anyhow, James is always off on business conferences. And you seem to manage pretty well without – "you know", as you call it.'

'Variety is the spice of life, my dear,' said Ginnie, and she glanced at Elaine through lowered lashes, 'And I should know.'

It took Elaine a few seconds to grasp her meaning. 'You're not - you're not saying what I think you're saying.'

'You are an innocent,' smiled Ginnie, moving closer to Elaine, so that they couldn't be heard. 'It doesn't hurt anyone. James is none the wiser. It makes a nice change from riding.'

'How do you know he won't find out?' said Elaine. 'You have no idea what it feels like to be on the receiving end of all that.'

It was difficult for her not to show how hurtful the words had been and she was aware that her face was giving away her emotions. She should have known her friend's nature from past times, but she'd imagined Ginnie's marriage to James was quite stable. She drew in a couple of deep breaths; she didn't want to start an argument. But Ginnie's attention was already elsewhere, as a tall figure came up behind her and put his hands over her eyes.

'Guess who?'

'Stephen, you idiot,' exclaimed Ginnie. 'Who else could it be?'

Elaine stood by as Stephen twirled his sister round and gave her a hug, saying, 'How are you, Ginnie? It's great to be home.' Elaine wondered if he'd remember her. But her unspoken thoughts were soon answered. 'And Elaine of the ginger pigtails. You've grown up.'

Elaine was aware of him casting a swift appreciative eye over her, and then, to her surprise, he grasped her too in a bear hug of an embrace.

Embarrassed, she struggled to regain her equilibrium.

'*Me* - grown up - you were a long-haired lout in oil-covered jeans when I last saw you.'

'Enough reminiscing, you two,' Ginnie broke in. 'Come and join the others and James will get you a sherry. I had hoped that Sally would come - you remember my little sister, Sally, don't you Elaine - but she rang and said she'd can't manage it after all. Stephen, she says why don't you pop over and see her tomorrow? She's having one of her famous parties.'

'Famous for what?' asked Stephen as James poured sherries from a heavy decanter.

'Notorious, I should say,' commented James. 'Notorious for cheap wine and a surplus of salt and vinegar crisps.'

Sherries consumed, Ginnie positioned them at the table. 'James, you must look after the ladies - the thorn between the roses, you might say.' Her lips twitched in the suspicion of a smile, as she directed Clare, a large, plain woman into a seat beside James. 'I'll sit next to Stephen, and Julian will be over here on the other side of me. That's what I like about a round table. It's so nice and cosy. We can all talk to each other.'

Elaine found herself sitting next to James on one side, and on the other, Julian, the florid faced husband of the un-rose-like Clare. Stephen sat opposite Elaine, and she did her best to deliver an equivalent amount of pleasantries to all of them.

Julian leaned across the table to address Stephen.

'Just back in England, I hear. No place like home, eh? How d'you get on with the Frogs?'

Elaine watched Stephen's face and noticed a scarcely perceptible tensing up of his jaw.

'Naturally, I'm glad to be back to see the family. But I enjoy being in France. Paris still holds a great deal of charm for me.'

'Well, each to his own, I suppose. I gave up all that foreign travel ten years ago, when I started working for James's firm. Had a desk job since then. And I'm damn thankful for that.' The man continued in the manner of a lecture, rather than a conversation. 'And frankly, I shall always be grateful that we're an island race - it's a pity that such a lot of - shall we say - refugees - seem to seek sanctuary here. I can see the day when we'll all be khaki coloured.'

Elaine, embarrassed, glanced at Stephen to see how he was going to react.

'I suppose it's feasible we could end up piebald or striped,' he replied, with a perfectly straight face. 'Just think what beautiful creatures zebras are.'

Elaine suppressed a laugh and cut a piece of her Ogen melon, since Ginnie, possibly to avert a souring of the conversation, had hurriedly told them to start.

The awkward moment passed as the pre-dinner sherries and the first glass of good wine removed tensions and improved humour. Clare, who had very little conversation, seemed intent on devouring her meal in the fastest possible time, whilst James and Stephen exchanged anecdotes about brushes with customs officials in their respective trips abroad.

'Did you see much of the French countryside?' Elaine asked her neighbour, hoping to have found a safe topic.

Ginnie, her face deadpan, murmured almost under her breath, 'Julian's always been interested in hills and lowlands, haven't you, Jules?' Taking a basket of bread rolls in her hand, she leaned towards him, her décolletage revealing to him more of her than was perhaps obvious to the rest of the table.

'Would you care for another roll, Julian?'

Raising one eyebrow imperceptibly, barely moving his eyes from the front of her dress, he took a roll in the palm of his hand and, with his thumb, gave it a slight squeeze, with the motion of one testing a peach for ripeness.

'That would give me great satisfaction.'

Elaine, astounded at this blatant by-play, glanced first at James, who was continuing his conversation, apparently totally unaware of these double entendres, and then at Stephen. Stephen too was speaking as though nothing was happening, but Elaine saw that his face had stiffened and there was an angry look in his eyes. She was relieved that she had not imagined the incident, inspired by her earlier conversation with Ginnie. Ginnie, who looked flushed and excited, was obviously enjoying the extra frisson, as she had put it, of conducting her flirtation under her husband's nose.

In a slight pause in the conversation, Clare came in, in a booming voice, 'Are you married, Stephen?'

'I haven't felt ready to make a commitment,' Stephen replied in a thinly veiled dig at his sister and her accomplice.

Julian, blissfully unaware of the coded message, joked, 'You needn't think marriage will tie you down, old chap. Sometimes the licence gives you extra licence.' And he roared with laughter at his own pun. Leaning across the table to his wife, once again engrossed in her meal, he shouted at her, 'Enjoying the *coq au vin*, old girl? That's one bird not ruling the roost, eh?'

The chicken was delicious. The company all concentrated on their food, murmuring only desultory conversation. Ginnie, glowing at the various compliments, looked remarkably pretty. Suddenly, Elaine felt a movement from her right-hand neighbour as he placed his hand on the hostess's thigh. Ginnie, not expecting the unsubtle approach at that moment jumped, and Stephen, jolted by her movement, half turned to see the misplaced hand. He glared at Julian.

Elaine glanced to see if he would say something but, in loyalty to his sister, he remained quiet. However in the lull, the incident had been more noticeable than had obviously been intended. James looked in the direction of his employee and at his wife, but his face gave away nothing.

'It's a strange thing how we mimic the animal world, I always feel, don't you, Julian?' he said. 'Now take what you were saying about that rooster on the plate there. It's chickens who invented the "pecking order", you know. But we bring it into our homes and we bring it into our businesses.'

'I always feel that we run a very democratic company,' said Julian, his voice a shade less confident.

'We do indeed. But there still has to be a managing director. There still has to be a decision maker at the top. And the same applies to the home.'

'Isn't that rather sexist? I never thought of you as the chauvinistic type,' said Elaine.

'I wouldn't say that I was chauvinistic, Elaine,' James replied. 'However, if, in a time of financial difficulties, I had to say to Ginnie, you're spending too much money on clothes, on entertaining or on the horses, surely, as the only breadwinner, that would be my right.'

Ginnie's face lost its rosy glow and she stared at James in surprised horror.

'I didn't think we had financial difficulties, have we?'

'Well, I'm speaking hypothetically, of course. But we've all suffered from the recession. The business has suffered. We may well have to contract our office staff. These days, with computers, there's less need for people pushing about bits of paper.'

Julian looked up quickly. His face, too, was changing colour and had taken on a yellowish sickly look. For a second, Elaine caught Stephen's eye and knew that they were both watching like an all-knowing, all-seeing theatre audience understanding the drama being played out, understanding the messages that James was pronouncing, and knowing that Ginnie and Julian were understanding them too. Elaine turned to see whether Clare was concerned, but she was giving her full attention to the chicken bone in her hand. She had obviously not taken in all the minutiae of the events of the past few minutes, and was barely listening to the conversation which, to all intents and purposes, had deteriorated into a financial and business discussion.

'In fact, I was sorry to hear you didn't care for travelling, Julian,' James continued. 'Because, unofficially, of course, I have a feeling that's where your future lies. We'll be needing more young computer literate people in the office. Well, of course that rules you out. But we do need your experience in the field. Selling to other countries while things are so difficult at home. And if it came to a choice of redundancy or travel, you might have to take on board a rather unpalatable decision.'

Elaine did not need to see Julian's reaction. Instead, she was focusing on James. His eyes, which she had always thought of as baby blue, were actually quite steely. No wonder he did so well in business. He must have been constantly under-estimated, to other people's cost.

'I've been watching the situation for some time now,' he added. 'And I think that's the way it must be.'

'Whereabouts were you thinking of?' Julian's voice sounded weak and subdued.

'Probably the Middle East. Saudi is on the cards. You'll have to be careful about the alcohol, of course. And don't put your hands on anything that doesn't belong to you. You know they have these rather fundamentalist ideas about morals. Stealing and adultery and so on.'

Elaine wondered what poetic justice he would now mete out to Ginnie. Would he threaten her with the loss of the dishwasher or the daily? Would he punish her by selling one of the horses? Or would he humiliate her, banish her, as he had Julian? But Ginnie, far from looking apprehensive, had recovered her glow and was looking at her husband with new respect.

'You know if there are problems, I'll do anything,' she said, with a soft girlish laugh, 'I'll be your willing slave.'

'I don't think we need consider anything too drastic,' he said and, looking directly at Ginnie, he allowed a slight smile to relax his face, whilst his eyes showed a flicker of amusement at her changed attitude.

The soufflé was served without a hitch.

Julian, looking nervous, managed to convey to his wife that she should abandon the plate of mints served with coffee and retire from the party. James, his hand resting on Ginnie's shoulder in a proprietary way, walked out into the hall to bid his guests goodbye, with the utmost courtesy.

Ginnie, still excited, like someone high on drugs or alcohol, talked too loudly outside the door. 'What's this ghastly red wine?' came her voice. 'I'll tell Stephen to take it to Sally's tomorrow night. He's brought a whole case of Le Montrachet, and we certainly don't need this cheap plonk.'

Elaine, not offended, giggled on hearing the fate of her mother's donation.

Ginnie came back to the table, as Stephen was pouring more coffee for Elaine and himself.

'Look, why don't you two take those out on the terrace? I think I'll call it a day. I've got a bit of a headache.' She bent to kiss her brother. 'James has already taken your case to your room, Elaine. Help yourself to brandies, won't you? I'll see you at breakfast.'

James put his head round the door to say goodnight to the two remaining guests, and then, with the door still ajar, they heard him say to his wife, 'I thought I heard a mention of that well known euphemism "the headache". I hope I got that wrong.'

Then, in a low voice, came Ginnie's reply. 'I told you - I'll be your willing slave.'

Elaine took a chocolate mint and tried not to look embarrassed. Stephen laughed and said, 'All she wanted was attention. She's always been like that. She'd behave as badly as she could, and usually rope someone else in too. Then she'd turn the charm on for Mum and Dad and get off scot-free.'

'Leaving someone else carrying the can?' queried Elaine.

'Yes. Right first time. Usually me. That's why I left home.'

'I thought that was because you got a place at university.'

'Yes, but once I was there, I made up my mind I wouldn't go back to living at home again. College life gave me more self-assurance, whereas sometimes your nearest and dearest sap your confidence – even when they don't mean to.'

'I know what you mean,' Elaine smiled, thinking of her own mother. 'But I thought you were quite confident. You and your pals and your bikes – you didn't seem to need anyone else; you seemed to enjoy yourselves.'

Her mind went back to her teenage years, when she had admired Ginnie's older brother as much as any rock star.

'Everyone has their own way of putting on an extra skin, haven't they?' he replied. 'For us it was overalls and an oil can. We didn't go clubbing and drinking - we were all a bit shy with girls.'

'I thought a motor cycle was the ultimate in phallic symbols.'

Stephen laughed. 'I didn't know that then. I don't think I could even spell it.'

'Lots of girls were interested in you.'

'I wish I'd known. I might have tried to date one of them. There was one girl I fancied. The very thought of asking her out made me shake with terror.'

'Girls can be unkind sometimes.'

'I'm sure she wouldn't have been unkind. It wasn't in her nature. I wish now I'd plucked up my courage.'

'What happened to her?'

'She got married. And now she's divorced.'

Elaine looked at him; his eyes smiled into hers, and she felt colour creeping into her cheeks. She got up and poured herself some brandy.

'My goodness. Aren't we getting sentimental, talking about our youth like this? When are you going back to France, Stephen?'

'Oh, didn't Ginnie tell you? I'm not going back. I'm bringing my so-called expertise here. It would be nice to get together, Elaine.'

Elaine looked doubtful and hesitated.

'I'm no carbon copy of Ginny,' he said, smiling but serious. 'I won't toy with your emotions. I'll even find some oily jeans if it will make you feel better.'

'Stephen, I'm not the same person you knew twelve years ago. As you said yourself, I'm divorced. I have a young child too.'

He took her hand in his, and his grip was firm.

'We're both grown-up people, now, Elaine. But you seem very much the same person to me. Honest, straightforward. Someone I'd very much like to know again.'

Elaine relaxed. She allowed her hand to remain in his. She couldn't deny that she felt very comfortable in his presence.

'Let's go out somewhere, tomorrow,' he said.

'I'm riding with Ginnie in the afternoon.'

'Well, after that, or before. What does it matter?'

She looked at the well-dressed young man. To all intents and purposes, there was very little left of the skinny youth of twelve years before, who, to her chagrin at that time, had seemed to have very little interest in her or any other girl. And yet beneath the exterior, she guessed that his old personality had remained intact. And somewhere, deep down, perhaps so too had hers. She felt a sudden awareness of the burden that she had become accustomed to carrying. Bringing up a young child, the responsibility of her job with its rigid deadlines - she was struck by a desire to shake off the years.

'You know what I'd like to do?' she said. 'I'd like to do something silly - like go to a fun fair, eat candy floss and drink coke from a can.'

He caught her mood in an instant. 'Then we could go on to Sally's party - we'd be just the right age for it - she's twenty-six, going on eighteen. We could take the awful wine and share their soggy crisps.' His eyes gleamed. 'We could go by bike.'

'You haven't still got that,' Elaine said incredulously.

She took a sip of James's best brandy and wondered if these things would really happen, or if they were inventing a dream.

'We'll tell Ginnie we'll be out for dinner,' Stephen continued.

'We could get fish and chips or a Chinese takeaway.'

'And we'd still have Sunday.'

It was going to be fun, she thought, two old friends revisiting their youth.

But from the touch of his hand and the tremor of her glass, she knew that they each shared the hope that it was going to be something more.

Chapter 12: Mother's Day

(Saturday evening)

Julie Stanton arrived back at her old home at six-thirty. It was a large Victorian house, which Sally Fairdene's parents had bought as an investment, and with the expectation that Sally would let out rooms to fellow students. The arrangement had worked well. Julie and the other lodgers who had rented at different times had been very comfortable, and there was no resentment about Sally's financially superior position.

Julie rang the doorbell and glanced at her watch. Fortunately, she was ahead of the party guests, for she was not really in the mood for socialising. Sally came to the door in a housecoat, wiping damp hair with a towel. Julie thought she saw a flicker of disappointment in her eyes, but in a flash it was replaced by a bright smile.

'Where have you been, Julie?' she said, dropping the towel and throwing her arms round her friend. 'Richard's been going out of his mind.'

'You know where I always end up when things go pear-shaped,' replied Julie, putting her small suitcase down in the hall. 'It didn't work out with Richard and me, as you obviously know, and I've been staying with Frank and Janet over the half term. But I've got school on Monday. So I wondered - have you let my room yet?'

'Don't be silly. I'm not that efficient. But why didn't you let Richard know? He's been trying to find you all week.'

'He couldn't have. I left messages with his mother.'

They exchanged glances.

'The old bat,' murmured Julie. 'Even so, perhaps it's all for the best. Do I really want to share my life with mother's blue-eyed boy? Surely there's some other sort of man apart from chauvinists or wimps.'

'Richard's not a wimp - you've misjudged him, Julie.' Sally looked down for a moment, before saying in a half laughing, half serious way, 'If you don't want him, I'll have him any day.'

Julie glanced at her in surprise, lost for words for the moment, before Sally added, 'Look, there's something else. Richard's sister's here.'

'What? She lives in Exeter.'

'Well, she's sitting in your room, crying her eyes out. You'd better go and talk to her. The regular crowd will be arriving in a couple of hours. And, what's more, I hear that my big brother is coming - maybe he's the man you're looking for. He deals in French wines and wears Saville Row suits - what more could a woman ask?'

Julie smiled, 'I think I need a bit of a respite.'

'The only problem is,' continued Sally, 'he's dragging along some old flame, would you believe? She's divorced now, with a kid. I think he's out of his mind. He's as eligible as can be - why does he want to put himself in that situation?'

'I don't want to get involved with your private grievances,' said Julie. 'I'd be as bad as Richard's mother, interfering old witch, wouldn't I?'

She picked up her bag and walked upstairs, preparing herself to confront a younger version of her adversary.

Pushing open the unlocked door, her eyes met those of a tall fair-haired girl, her face blotched with tears.

'You must be Elizabeth...'

'Yes, I'm Liz, Richard Webb's sister,' agreed the girl. 'Who are you?'

'I'm Julie. I thought you wanted to see me.'

'Oh, your friend, Sally, said she didn't know when you'd be back.' Liz blew her nose hard, but fresh tears ran down her cheeks.

'You look terrible,' Julie said, concerned. 'Let me make you some tea or coffee. Things can't be that bad.'

This tearful girl was obviously not a clone of her mother. On the contrary, though she was several inches taller than Julie, the only way to deal with her, in the absence of information, was to treat her like a member of Julie's infant class with a hurt knee. Julie fussed around, made a drink, took Liz's coat and hung it up; then turned the heating on to take the chill off the unused bed-sit. Eventually, Liz looked more settled.

'What made you come here? I thought you lived in Exeter.'

'I came to London to sort things out with Mother, but she wouldn't speak to me; she didn't even say where Richard was. But Sally told me he would probably come tonight. She said she'd try and get in touch with him.'

Julie, initially surprised, considered this for a moment. The story still seemed complicated, but some things were beginning to add up and, on balance, she was not so surprised.

'So Richard wasn't at his flat, then?' she said.

'No, I rang the flat from the station, and Mother wouldn't speak to me. I wanted to persuade her to come back home, but she wouldn't listen to a word I said. She said she had two ungrateful children and there was no point in talking to either of us.' She blew her nose hard. 'When she put the phone down on me, I remembered I had your number in my diary. Richard gave it to me some time back. I rang up and Sally told me how to get here.'

'What do you want to do now?' asked Julie.

'Well, if I could contact Richard, at least he could sort me out somewhere to stay - I can't go back to the flat. And I can't face going back to Exeter tonight.'

'Well, you can stay here, if that's the only problem,' said Julie. 'I'll make up the bed. Both beds. I didn't expect to be here myself.'

Liz, still sniffing, looked curious. 'Don't you live here any more?

'Actually, I was about to move into Richard's flat, when your mother came for her visit from Exeter. And that put paid to that. Perhaps it wasn't meant to happen.'

'So you didn't really want Mother around,' said Liz.

'I think you could say that your mother arriving when she did certainly did not enhance our situation. I walked out in a huff. But I thought it was only a postponement of our plans. I thought Richard would ring me the next day. Now I wonder if it's too late to repair what's already happened - he doesn't seem very anxious to get me back into his life. Although...' The suspicions that formulated in her mind remained unsaid, but Richard's mother had predictably failed to pass on messages, and Sally hadn't exactly assisted Richard to find her. 'Well, let's not worry about that for the moment,' she said. 'How about you? You said you had a row with your mum. What made you decide to eat humble pie?'

'I miss Mother. She's such a rock to have around, especially now.'

'Why now?'

'I'm pregnant.'

'Oh, that's why you're so weepy. And your mother left you. Doesn't she like children?'

'She didn't know. I wanted to be sure, because I've had a miscarriage before. But I was awfully jumpy. Then we had a trivial row about something. I just shouted at her once, and she got on her high horse and walked out.'

'She's very dignified, your mother. I can imagine she wouldn't like being shouted at.'

'How right you are. She absolutely hates "displays of temperament", as she puts it. But sometimes it's very difficult keeping your temper with Mother. She's enough to try the patience of a saint. And she's got a very low opinion of Gary.'

Julie couldn't help looking a bit puzzled. 'Well, if you see all those faults in her, why on earth do you want her back?'

Liz smiled a tearful smile. 'I know she must seem absolutely awful to you, Julie. She gives a very bad first impression and always comes over as a rather cold person. But you see, I know what she's been through. She lost Dad when we were very young - and she really adored him. She was very proud and we had a lot of financial difficulties. Her mother was dead and her father didn't help her, because he'd never approved of Dad. You'd think, after that, she wouldn't want to make the same mistake with Gary. Anyway, she just struggled on, making ends meet, until her father died and left her a lot of money. She was very possessive, because Richard and I were all she'd got. And then of course, it followed that no-one was good enough for her two wonderful children.'

'Did she ever make it up with her father?'

'No. She didn't know he'd forgiven her until the reading of his will.'

'Oh, how awful to be so proud. Have you and Richard inherited that gene?'

'I hope I'm always prepared to back down rather than lose the people I love,' said Liz. 'I just wish Mother would give me the chance.'

Julie thought for a moment. 'Liz, I'm sure your mother would want to be back in Exeter when you have your baby. But isn't there a danger that she'll want to take that over too? Are you sure you will always want her to be quite so closely involved in bringing up your baby?'

'I shall have to be very strong-minded. But I can't think of anything more dreadful than her being isolated from both of us. She can't manage things properly in Richard's flat. She's got arthritis and she needs to be in her own home. Of course I want her around when I have the baby. But she needs me too. She's just too proud to admit it to herself.'

'Perhaps it would help if I spoke to her,' said Julie. 'If you don't mind me making you sound more helpless than you are, she might feel that she could go back home without losing her dignity.'

'It's worth a try,' Liz replied.

Picking up the phone, Julie dialled the flat. Violet Webb, it appeared, was prepared to answer the telephone.

'Mrs Webb. It's Julie Stanton here again. Please don't put the phone down. I'm not going to ask you to pass on any more of my messages to Richard. I'm aware of your disapproval of me and you can congratulate yourself on successfully putting the kybosh on our relationship.'

'I don't know what you're talking about,' came the distant tones of Violet Webb.

'This is not about Richard. It's about your daughter.'

'Elizabeth?' came the startled response.

'I have something very important to say about Elizabeth. She's come here in a very unhappy state.'

'What do you mean – here? My daughter's in Exeter.'

'No. She's with me now and she's quite distraught, and that's not a good thing in her condition.'

There was a moment's pause, as Violet obviously took in the significant phrase.

'Condition?'

'Your daughter is pregnant, and she didn't know how to tell you, when you were so angry.'

'Pregnant?' Violet sounded stunned, 'You're saying that my daughter is pregnant?

'Yes. She's here with me now.'

Violet's voice was faint. 'Why didn't she say? Why didn't she tell me? She knows how important it is. We've all been waiting - hoping...'

'She wanted to talk to you. She wanted to be with you. I can't believe you would have treated her as you did, if you had realised. But if you don't want her there, I'll make up a bed for her tonight.'

'Stuff and nonsense,' said Violet Webb, sounding to Julie like the Red Queen. 'She must come back here at once. She shouldn't be chasing around the countryside in that state. I can't understand why she didn't tell me.'

'She tried to tell you. You were very angry. You were angry about me and Richard. But Liz has nothing to do with that. And Richard and I are probably finished now anyway.'

'My dear Julie. I've never heard such rubbish. He's made it abundantly clear that his life is here with you. I can't imagine why you're giving up on him. He's such a loving boy. And he thinks very highly of you.'

I'm no longer a threat, Julie thought. I don't even matter to her any more. But she couldn't help expressing the feelings that had buzzed through her head in the past few days.

'I can't believe that's true, or he wouldn't have let me go so easily. Maybe it's better for all of us that we call a halt to it.'

'Perhaps it's you that's given up too easily. Perhaps you just don't care for him enough to try. I can tell you, when I met the man for me, I didn't give up. Richard and Elizabeth wouldn't be here today if I had.' Her voice shook slightly. 'And no-one can replace *him*.'

For a moment Julie was silent at the confirmation of what Liz had already said. The old girl was vulnerable, after all. And, perhaps without realising it, she had clung on to Richard as a replacement for his dead father.

Violet Webb's voice softened for a moment.

'My daughter - she is all right, isn't she?'

'Yes, she is,' replied Julie.

'Tell her to come back, here. I'll go back to Exeter with her tomorrow. She must look after herself. This baby is too important to take chances.'

'I'll tell her.'

Julie put down the phone. She turned to Liz. 'It's all OK. You don't have to stay here. She wants to take you home. Shall I call you a taxi?'

Liz was already gathering up her things.

They walked down the stairs together to wait for the cab. One or two people drifted through the open front door, greeting Julie as they passed.

'Thank you for all your help, Julie,' said Liz. 'I do hope everything turns out all right between you and Richard. I'm sure you'll be a good friend - and I hope, at some time, auntie to my little one.'

Julie looked down at her toes, avoiding Liz's eyes.

'I'm afraid there's not much permanence amongst our crowd,' she said, giving a casual wave in the direction of another party guest.

A motor cycle roared past, its black clad driver and passenger almost touching the ground, as it turned the corner. They slowed to a stop a few yards away and exchanged words before the passenger dismounted and started walking towards the house. Julie stared at the unknown figure, who walked past her through the doorway.

'You see how it is,' she said to Liz. 'People arrive - I don't even know them. We're chopping and changing all the time. It seems like Sally's cooking up plans to take over Richard and, as for me, well, there'll be someone else.'

'You don't fool me, Julie,' said Liz. 'I don't think you're really so flippant. And as for Sally - she's not right for him. Don't give up on him.'

'Look, there's your taxi,' said Julie, as a cab rounded the corner. She took Liz's bag and walked to the roadside. 'Take care of yourself - and that baby.'

Liz gave Julie a spontaneous hug before getting into the cab, and Julie waved as it moved away into the traffic. Out of the corner of her eye, she saw the motor cycle which had just gone past pulling into a parking space further up the road, and the driver dismounting and adjusting the stand. She didn't recognise the figure at all, and hoped that the two bikers did not represent trouble.

She climbed the stairs to the first floor, and went into the kitchen. Someone had left a bottle of wine on the kitchen table, with a vaguely familiar motif. She took a closer look and, to her astonishment, saw emblazoned on the label, 'J loves R'.

'That's my bottle of wine,' she exclaimed.

Chapter 13: Wine and Roses

(Saturday night)

Julie was intrigued. Who was the present owner of the bottle of wine? She decided to get changed and join the party.

She went up to her room, found a black culotte skirt and top and wandered back downstairs to the kitchen. It was getting late and many of the regular Saturday night crowd had begun to arrive, bringing bottles and depositing them in the kitchen. Julie tucked away 'her' bottle into a corner, so that it would be unlikely to be anyone's first choice. She looked around, but saw no clue as to its donor. How could it possibly have travelled from Barry's house, where Frank and Janet had taken it? She couldn't imagine either of her brothers coming to a party here. Neither of them had ever fitted in with her friends. Even as she pondered, she knew she would never get a satisfactory answer to the question.

The house was a typical town house with only two or three rooms on each floor, but it no longer bore the hallmarks of student accommodation. Nonetheless, many of the guests had graduated from that era - some from Julie and Sally's art college days, wearing fairly outlandish arty crafty gear. Others were from the advertising agency where Sally now worked, and were casually smart, contrasting with Sally's own individualist style, her shift-like garment dressed up with lots of chains around her neck and long earrings clinking backwards and forwards at each movement.

There were tureens of spaghetti with Bolognese sauce and Sally had left it to her friends to help themselves.

Julie stood, feeling rather disconsolate, ladling some pasta on to a plate, and thought again of the occasion, only a week ago, that she and Richard had shared a similar meal, before the unexpected arrival of his mother.

A woman came into the kitchen, carrying a heavy crash helmet. Her auburn hair was untidy and she wore a masculine leather jacket.

Julie tensed, realising that this was the stranger she had seen downstairs. She cast a chilly look in the intruder's direction. They were always concerned at the possibility of gatecrashers but, when the woman spoke, her voice was gentle and pleasant. 'Is there somewhere I can tidy up and leave these things?'

'Of course. I'll take you to one of the bedrooms. Are you a friend of Sally or Sue?'

'Sally,' murmured the woman, as Julie led the way to a bedroom. 'My name's Elaine.'

Julie introduced herself, found a space for the crash helmet and leather jacket and stood whilst Elaine patted her hair into place.

'My - friend, Stephen Fairdene - he's parking the bike,' Elaine continued. 'He's Sally's brother.'

Julie thought about the other biker she had seen. 'Saville Row suits,' she murmured.

'I beg your pardon?'

'It's OK - just thinking aloud. I'm sorry. I must have seemed a bit unwelcoming earlier. It's just that you have to be so careful here in central London. Strangers can come into a party and start circulating drugs and all sorts.'

They wandered back into the kitchen.

'Of course. And I can assure you I didn't lace the bottle of wine with LSD or anything.'

'Bottle of wine?' queried Julie.

'Yes. I put it down here - oh someone's moved it. Not that it was anything special; just a bottle of plonk.'

'Funny you should say that. It was rather special actually,' said Julie, taking the bottle from its corner. 'You see it was my wine. I mean it was before I gave it to someone - look, see my initials and my boyfriend's – "J loves R".

'Well, that bottle certainly must have been around,' smiled Elaine. 'Now I come to think of it, my dad said he won it at a tombola. And now it's back to you.'

'It seems almost like a sign from someone up there. If you don't mind, I think I'll hide it away again.'

A noise erupted from the entrance hall below. It sounded like an argument. The two women exchanged glances. Raised voices were followed by the thud of someone falling heavily. Then a plaintive squeak from the hostess, 'You idiots - that's my brother.'

Julie and Elaine left the kitchen to meet Sally and a bruised Stephen climbing the stairs to the landing.

Elaine looked horrified at the emerging black eye.

'Are you all right?' she asked.

'You should have seen the other guy,' said Stephen with a good-natured laugh. 'I don't think much of Sally's greeting though. Sending the heavy mob to sort me out.'

'They thought you were a gatecrasher. Who can blame them? What's all this leather gear for?' Sally asked.

'Elaine and I are wearing the correct protective clothing for travelling on a motor cycle,' replied Stephen with dignity.

'You're not still riding a motor bike! You could afford a Porsche!' exclaimed Sally.

'This is not just *a* motorbike. It's *the* motorbike. When I give up riding my Harley Davidson, you'll know I've reached middle age.'

'We ought to do something about your eye, Stephen,' Sally said. 'There's a nasty gash at the side. Julie'll sort it out for you. She knows all about first aid.' She glanced around the room to see who else was coming in. 'Sorry, I didn't introduce you. Though it's a bit late now. Julie, my flat-mate; Stephen, my brother.'

Julie didn't think much of the welcome Sally was extending to her brother, who had been out of the country for years, but he seemed a nice guy. She smiled at him. 'Come into the kitchen, and I'll bathe your eye, Stephen.'

Sally turned to Elaine, who was hovering, 'And I'm afraid I didn't catch the name of your biker friend.'

'This is Elaine,' said Stephen, 'She's the editor of a woman's mag. What's it called, Elaine? Upfront Woman?'

'Forward Woman.'

Sally looked impressed. 'Really? Their art work is so good. Look, you must come and meet some of my friends from art college. They've got all sorts of ideas.'

And Sally had ideas too, thought Julie, as she sat Stephen down in the kitchen and observed Elaine being led, rather reluctantly, away. Ideas about Julie and Stephen. Ideas about Richard and Sally.

Stephen smiled at Julie, 'I feel embarrassed to be on the receiving end of this tender loving care,' he said, as Julie wiped away an antiseptic tear that ran down the side of his face. 'Won't your boyfriend object?'

'He's not around at the moment. We have a problem. A mother.'

Stephen almost had to shout as the general hubbub from the other room rose before subsiding again.

'Did you say "another"? Another woman?'

'Yes. His mother.'

'A formidable rival. It's taken years abroad to separate me from mine. After all, it is the first intimate relationship that most men have.'

'You're a psychologist.'

'No, a wine importer. I'm just interested in relationships. My mother always made it clear she preferred her two pretty daughters to her messy little boy. She didn't seem to realise I was her greatest fan. I would have done anything for her. Well, at ten, anyway. Ouch, that stuff stings.'

'Yes, eau de TCP. Not the most alluring of after-shaves.' said Julie as the buzz of conversation once again drowned out the words.

'Not stinks, stings,' he repeated, laughing.

'Sorry,' said Julie, reaching in the first aid box for a plaster. 'Be thankful my first aid doesn't extend to tetanus jabs or penicillin in the backside. Well, at least your mother problems stopped at ten. Richard's still having his.'

'I wouldn't say my problems were over then. It's only since I've taken myself away from the scene and viewed it from across a stretch of water that I've been able to get it into perspective. All I'm saying is - don't be too hard on your boyfriend. Don't put him in a position where he has to make choices.'

'You're a nice man,' said Julie, and patted the plaster on to the wound. 'If Sally had introduced you to me before I met Richard, I'd have been seriously interested.' She gave him a light kiss on the cheek.

'Julie!' There was an irate roar from the landing. They both turned.

Richard marched into the kitchen, his face dark and angry.

'Richard. I didn't know you were coming here.'

'That's obvious,' he said, the words hardly able to escape from his gritted teeth. 'What kind of a woman are you, Julie? You run away from what I thought was something special and in one week you're flirting with someone else.' He turned his attention to Stephen. 'Who the hell are you?'

Those guests now overflowing onto the landing quietened down at this additional excitement. Elaine, hovering at the edge, looked concerned.

Stephen raised his hands to protect his face. 'I can assure you I'm simply a patient here, with no wish to sustain any more injuries. Have English men got more aggressive since I left?' he murmured half to himself. 'Let me call my lady to verify. Elaine,' he called, 'Come and rescue me from an enraged lover.'

The spectators turned to watch with increased interest. Elaine came over, laughing, and Richard and Julie stood blushing with embarrassment at the attention.

'We'll leave you two to sort out your problems,' said Stephen, getting up. 'I have the feeling that we're standing in the middle of an erupting volcano, and it's not due to our stoking.'

Richard, his face now even more flushed, mumbled something, extending a hand to Stephen.

Stephen shook hands and gave Julie a peck on the cheek. 'See you around some time. Get your crash helmet, Elaine. Let's get the bike and go back to the dodgems. Sally's parties are a bit too energetic for me.'

The couple linked hands and walked to the stairs.

'I've never heard you get angry before, Richard,' said Julie in a low voice. 'Didn't think I was that important.'

'Not important? I've spent most of the week looking for you. And when I find you, you're chatting up someone else.'

'Don't be angry, Richard. I wasn't chatting him up; he was just a kind, understanding man. But I can't understand why you couldn't find me. Didn't you realise I might be with Frank?'

'Sally looked for the number, but she couldn't lay her hands on it.

Julie glanced up, a slight smile on her lips. Another confirmation of Sally's intentions.

'And he's ex-directory,' Richard continued. 'I tried your other brother several times, and it was always on answer-phone. There was a cryptic message like, "Barry and Linda are having fun. Please try later."'

'How strange,' said Julie. 'Fun's not a word I'd associate with Barry and Linda.'

'Well you try them if you don't believe me,' said Richard, still sounding angry. 'I left lots of messages, but they didn't reply. I only came tonight, because Sally said you were almost certain to be here.'

'Did she?' murmured Julie, 'And, of course, she was right. Here I am. What about your mother? Did she tell you I rang?'

Richard glowered. 'No, she did not. But in any case, she stopped talking to me after last Sunday.'

'Why, what did you do?'

'I moved out. I told her she was very welcome to stay in the flat as long as she wanted, but it wasn't my intention to be there too. Then I moved into a hotel.'

'You left her on her own?'

'Look, I know her kind of moral blackmail. I couldn't do much about it on Saturday night, could I? You thought I was being weak, but you weren't entirely innocent. You were only too ready to be offended. You'd made up your mind to go before I could think it through.'

'She was making me feel uncomfortable,' Julie blurted out. 'Deliberately.'

'I understood that. That's why I let you go. But I wasn't going to let her win. At least - the battle, but not the war.'

'Richard, can we stop being angry with each other?'

He smiled and his face relaxed. 'Of course we can.'

'Then I've got something to tell you. Your mother's going home.'

'Really? How do you know that?'

'Your sister, Liz, has been here today. She came to London especially to take your mother home. And you're going to be an uncle.'

Richard beamed with pleasure. 'That's great news.'

'And your mother doesn't care about us any more. This horrible week was all for nothing.'

'What does that matter? We're together now.'

'Are we, Richard? Is our relationship strong enough?'

'Julie. We can survive a few angry words. No-one can love you more than I do. Compared to that, what does a week matter?'

'I thought I'd lost you,' Julie said, his words bringing tears to her eyes. She was herself again in a moment; she had no reason to be tearful. 'But you're right. All I lost was a week. We could have had such a good time, though, if only you'd managed to get hold of me. We could have slept in a four-poster, with curtains all the way round. We could have had breakfast in bed. What fun we could have had. What a waste of the half term holiday.'

'It's not really that sort of hotel. But we could go there just the same. I'm still booked in.'

'Oh let's do that. And you know what? We could take our bottle of wine. I lost it, then I found it again. I knew it was symbolic.'

Richard, amused, picked it up. 'Well, what do you know? Come on then. Let's go and say goodbye to Sally.'

'Oh, Richard,' Julie said, preparing to lie, 'Don't kiss Sally. She's got a cold sore.'

'Really, I didn't notice.'

He's so innocent, thought Julie, he shouldn't be allowed out on his own. Still, he'd dealt with the old dragon, and that must have taken some doing.

They arrived at the Hotel London Berkeley, where no nightingales sang. It was a small business hotel, with a very correct desk clerk at Reception.

Julie, modern woman though she was, was nevertheless ready to slink up the back stairs.

Richard, however, approached the desk.

'My friend is staying the night,' he said without a blush, 'and I'd like to change my room. Can I take over the bridal suite?'

The desk clerk looked startled.

'I'm afraid we have no such room, sir.' Then he relented a little and a gently amused smile crossed his face. 'But I can let you have a nice double room overlooking the square. I'll get the porter to take up madam's luggage.'

'Madam hasn't got any luggage,' Richard told him. He took out his wallet. 'Just send up a bottle of champagne - and some flowers. You can put it on the bill.'

'And your belongings from your other room, sir.'

'Just leave them outside the door.'

'It's Room 28, sir. Will that be all?'

'That'll be all.' He took the key from the clerk and passed him a ten pound note. 'Thanks for your help.'

Julie totally awed by this new aspect of Richard, followed him silently to the elevator. They stood looking at each other in the small claustrophobic space without saying anything.

They arrived on the second floor, and Richard took Julie's hand, the key pressing hard into her palm, and propelled her to the room, only releasing his grip as they stood at the entrance. He still clasped the bottle of wine in his other hand, almost oblivious to it.

He unlocked the door and held it open for Julie, his eyes following her, and as she walked in, she half turned toward him.

'I've missed you,' she said.

Once inside the room, he clicked the door shut, and put down the wine.

A while later, a porter tapped on the door.

'Room service, sir.'

He tapped again but got no reply. Shrugging his shoulders, he put the bottle of champagne and a dozen roses, acquired with great difficulty at that time on a Saturday night, on the floor outside the door. When he returned an hour later with a suitcase containing Richard's belongings, they were still there.

Forthcoming Goldenford books

Anne Brooke - *Café Society*

Angie Soames is determined to leave her home in the idyllic Essex countryside and set up her own café in London, but before she can achieve her goal she has to overcome potential disasters in the shape of a glamorous French waiter, a grouchy German chef and her transvestite uncle.

And, if she manages to keep the lid on all that, what will she do about the other hidden secrets of her family?

Mike Hall - *Haven*

Futuristic thriller in which Glanda, a beautiful alien, appears from nowhere seeking help. Her fishnet stockings initially spark a fashion frenzy but later cause a worldwide crisis. In the chaos, babies are conceived and all is laid bare. Can Chu Min, Karin and Jo save the world with Glanda's help? Will Glanda be allowed to leave? To find out, you must read this story of greed, intrigue and sex.

Jennifer Margrave - *The Priedeux trilogy*

Priedeux – a character who changes the course of history …

In the first book, Priedeux sets out for the wilds of Wirral on a quest to discover the writer of *Gawain and the Green Knight*, a seditious poem with a hidden agenda - a call to rebellion against Richard II. Can Priedeux find the writer in time to stop the rebellion and save his own life?

The second novel focuses on Anne Boleyn and her political and personal machinations and the third reveals that Marlowe did not die at Deptford but enjoys a riotous life involving carnival in Rome, a shipwreck and sojourns in Florence and Venice…and using his experiences to weave new plays of Shakespearean stature.

And, once Priedeux has 'found himself' in his own quest, he accompanies the other main characters - as mentor, commentator and sometime critic.

Also available from Goldenford

Esmé Ashford - *On the Edge*

Tramps with bad feet, a sheep rustler, a busker invited to dinner; a weird monster who devours a nasty husband and a child who learns from a visit to the fun fair; limericks and blank verse; it is all here.

Irene Black – *The Moon's Complexion*

Bangalore, India 1991. Ashok Rao, a young doctor, has returned home from England to choose a bride.

But who is the intriguing Englishwoman who seeks him out? Why is she afraid and what is the secret that binds them together?

The lives of two strangers are turned upside down when they meet and the past comes to haunt them. *The Moon's Complexion* is a tale of love across cultural boundaries. It is also a breath-taking adventure tale played out in the mystical lands of Southern India and Sri Lanka and in the icy countryside of winter England.

info@goldenford.co.uk

www.goldenford.co.uk